Cooper's Story

A Puppy Tale

Also by
W. Bruce Cameron

A PUPPY TALE

Cooper's Story

W. Bruce Cameron

Illustrations by
Richard Cowdrey

STARSCAPE

A Tom Doherty Associates Book
New York

COOPER'S STORY

Copyright © 2021 by W. Bruce Cameron
Illustrations © 2021 by Richard Cowdrey
Reader's guide copyright © Tor Books

A Starscape Book
Published by Tom Doherty Associates
120 Broadway
New York, NY 10271

www.tor-forge.com

Library of Congress Cataloging-in-Publication Data

Names: Cameron, W. Bruce, author. | Cowdrey, Richard, illustrator.
Title: Cooper's story : a puppy tale / W. Bruce Cameron ;
illustrations by Richard Cowdrey.
Description: First edition. | New York : Starscape,
a Tom Doherty Associates Book, 2021.
Identifiers: LCCN 2021008850 (print) | LCCN 2021008851 (ebook) |
ISBN 9781250163387 (hardcover) | ISBN 9781250163370 (ebook)
Subjects: LCSH: Dogs—Juvenile fiction. | CYAC: Dogs—Fiction. | Animals—
Infancy—Fiction. | Service dogs—Fiction. | Human-animal relationships—Fiction. |
People with disabilities—Fiction. | Wheelchairs—Fiction.
Classification: LCC PZ10.3.C1466 Co 2021 (print) |
LCC PZ10.3.C1466 (ebook) | DDC [Fic]—dc23
LC record available at https://lccn.loc.gov/2021008850
LC ebook record available at https://lccn.loc.gov/2021008851

Our books may be purchased in bulk for promotional, educational, or business use.
Please contact your local bookseller or the Macmillan Corporate and Premium
Sales Department at 1-800-221-7945, extension 5442, or by email
at MacmillanSpecialMarkets@macmillan.com.

First Edition: June 2021

Printed in the United States of America

0 9 8 7 6 5

As I write this, teachers the world over
are struggling to help students stay on track
during virtual learning and school closures.

This novel is dedicated to those hardworking,
brave educators.

Thank you for helping students love to read!

Cooper's Story

A Puppy Tale

1

I lived with my puppy brothers and sisters and Mother Dog. I had a human friend named Ava, and best of all, I had a dog friend named Lacey.

Lacey was the best playmate any dog ever had. This was something I knew the moment I met her, that we were destined to be together forever.

My littermates were like me, with thick grayish-white fur, but Lacey, who was my age, had a somewhat pushed-in snout; very short, coarse fur; and white on her face. My siblings seemed to feel Lacey was too different from us to play with, which was fine by me—I wanted her all to myself, anyway.

Lacey always wanted to do everything I wanted to do. She would spring on me and start wrestling at precisely the right moment. She knew the game Pin Your

Friend Down and Chew on His Ears and would play it with me until it was time to do something else. She knew how to grab a ball and run with it and let it fall out of her mouth so that it bounced between her paws. Then I'd lunge for it and she'd try to get it and whoever snatched up that ball with their teeth would run and run and run some more while Ava laughed and clapped.

All my littermates knew how to do was grab the ball and keep it to themselves.

There were lots of dogs where we lived, in pens of their own. Very few were puppies. The place was loud with their barking. They barked for attention. They barked because they were inside and wanted to go out. They barked because other dogs were barking.

None of them mattered to me—only Lacey. When we were all let out into the yard, I would stand still with my nose in the air until I found her scent. When I slept in my own pen with my mother and brothers and sisters, Lacey and I wrestled in our dreams.

"I think Lacey is your one true love, Cooper," Ava told me.

I didn't understand what Ava was saying, but I loved hearing my name and Lacey's name at the same time. It meant that Ava knew Lacey and I belonged together.

One day, Ava and Lacey and I were playing in the yard. Lacey had one end of a stick in her mouth, so I

grabbed the other end. We tugged each other around the yard, giving mock growls.

Ava giggled when the stick broke and Lacey staggered back. I ran to get a drink from the water bowl, and Lacey bounded over to me and jumped on me so my face was dunked in the bowl. I backed out and shook, and then I ran over to Ava to get some petting.

Lacey followed me for the same reason. Ava was very good at petting. Her fingers knew right where to scratch, along my chest and right at the base of my tail.

"Lots of people have true loves," Ava told me as she gently scratched. "So I don't see why dogs shouldn't. Even puppies. You've always loved Lacey, Cooper. That's why Dad makes sure you get to play together every day."

I liked the way Ava smelled—sweet and spicy and flowery all at once. I crawled into her lap. Lacey climbed on top of me and sat on me until I shook her off. Ava lay back, and we all rolled around together in the grass.

"I bet I've got a true love, too, somewhere," Ava whispered. "I bet I'll find him one day."

I grabbed another stick and ran around the yard so that Lacey would chase me. Which of course she did.

Lacey and I would be together always. Somehow, deep inside, I knew this to be true.

We weren't together every single moment, of course. When we left the yard and Ava led us inside, she put me in my pen with my family, and Lacey was in her pen with hers.

I slept happily, piled in a heap with my furry brothers and sisters, dreaming of playing with Lacey.

One morning, Ava and Dad arrived very early to feed us. I knew something unusual was going on, because they were both excited—Ava especially. Her excitement hummed off her skin. It made her voice high and eager.

"Adoption fair day!" she told my littermates and me after she poured food in our bowls. We surged forward to gobble it up. I had a lot of brothers and sisters—too many, in my opinion—and they all liked to eat just as much as I did. I had to shove Heavy Boy away from my bowl, and while I was doing that, White-Face Sister pushed her face where mine had been. She was always doing that. Black-Tail and White-Tail Sisters ate from the same bowl, as they usually did, and Grumpy Brother got a bowl all his own because he was not good at sharing.

I kept my eye on Heavy Boy, because after he'd eaten more than anybody else, he had a habit of seeking me out and sitting on my head. That's why I thought of him as Heavy Boy.

"You'll all have new homes!" Ava told us as we ate. I wagged up at her because I knew she was happy.

After breakfast and outside time with Lacey, we were put into our crates. Surely that was not what Ava and Dad were excited about. There is nothing especially thrilling about crate time. It is nice for napping, though, so that's what I did, lying on top of Heavy Boy, which was so much more comfortable than the other way around.

The crate moved and jolted, which was strange. Crates did not normally do that. But I did not really feel like opening my eyes and investigating, so I just curled up tighter and slept deeper until all the jolting stopped.

Then all the grown-up dogs started barking. I heard Lacey yip, and I barked along with all the other dogs because if it was time for barking, I didn't want to be left behind. I didn't know *why* we were barking, just that we were barking.

"Settle down now!" Dad said. "Come on, Ava, let's get the crates out of the pickup."

Dad and Ava and some other humans I did not know picked up our crates and carried them a little way before setting them down. I looked around with interest.

We were outside, in the biggest yard I'd ever seen. I could not even catch sight of a fence, that's how big it was. Dad and Ava and their helpers arranged all the crates in the grass. Lacey's crate was next to mine, and I pressed close to the side of my crate so I could be near her. She did the same thing, and we touched noses through the cold wires and whined a little at each other, partly out of nervousness, partly out of longing to get free of our crates and play and wrestle in the big, wide grass.

I couldn't bear to be separated from Lacey. We were supposed to be together, always. Ava knew this, and I expected her to let us out of our crates so we could run in this wonderful, huge yard. The other dogs could stay in their crates, especially my brother Heavy Boy. Let him sit on somebody else besides me. Lacey and I needed to be let out to play and play.

But that didn't happen. I was surprised at Ava and Dad. Usually, they understood dogs very well, but they didn't seem to understand that we needed to explore this new yard. Instead, they were very busy talking with lots of new people who were walking around and looking in all the crates and petting all the dogs.

A man and a woman came by our crate, and the man crouched down to look at us. "They're adorable! What breed?" he asked.

"Mostly malamute, I think," Dad told them. "Maybe some Dane, too."

"Going to be pretty big, then, huh?" the man asked. "We've got a small apartment, and there's no yard."

"Malamutes need room to run," Dad said. "Let me show you some of our other pups."

Dad walked away with the man. I looked over at

Lacey and saw that a girl was peering into her crate. She smelled a little older than Ava, and she had long, shiny dark hair that spread out across her back.

"Oh, you are the prettiest baby. You are so beautiful," she whispered. She poked her fingers through the wires of Lacey's crate, and for once, Lacey wasn't paying attention to me. She licked the girl's fingers and looked up at her with adoration. The girl gazed back with just the same kind of love in her face.

Ava was nearby, smiling. "That's Lacey. My dad says she is probably spaniel mixed with something bigger, like boxer or Labrador," she told the girl.

"She's the one I want," the girl replied.

Ava opened the door of Lacey's crate, and the girl reached in and picked Lacey up, plopping her into her lap. Lacey squirmed and wiggled and put two paws on the girl's chest so she could lick her under the chin. There was a lot of giggling, and Lacey's tail wagged hard.

I could tell that this girl was nice. And she loved Lacey already. That was good! I pawed at my crate impatiently so that Ava would let me out, too. We could all play—Lacey and this new girl and me.

The girl swept Lacey up and rubbed her face on the top of Lacey's head. "Yes, she's the one!" she declared happily.

Ava was grinning. "Your mom and dad can fill out all the paperwork over there," she said, pointing.

"Thanks!" The girl stood up and shook her long black hair out of her face. She turned and walked away.

She walked away carrying Lacey!

I jumped up. I barked. Something very strange and wrong was happening here. The girl was going somewhere with Lacey and leaving me behind!

Lacey, too, seemed to realize that something was wrong. She put her face over the girl's shoulder, poking her nose through the curtain of sleek, dark hair. She stared at me as the girl carried her away, and I stared at her.

What was happening? Where was Lacey going?

Come back!

But Lacey did not come back. Before long, I couldn't even *see* her.

I could not help myself—I cried and whined and yipped. I was frantic. Where was Lacey? I pushed my nose through the holes in the crate and sniffed, trying to find her scent as it faded away. Then I pawed at the sides of the crate, frantic to get out. I had to go find her! Didn't any of the humans who were smiling down at me understand how wrong this was?

Ava was drawn by my crying. "Oh, Cooper. You miss Lacey, don't you?" She poked her fingers in, and I licked them desperately. "Don't worry, you're going to have a people family of your own!"

I thought if she said Lacey's name, it meant Ava was

9

going to take me to her, but I heard Dad call, "Ava!" and she left at a run.

After a long time, I turned away. Upset, I lay down and shoved my face into Mother Dog's flank. She licked my head, which was a little comfort. But I wanted Lacey, and she was not there.

For as long as I could remember, Lacey and I had been together. More than any of my littermates, she was the one I cared about. I belonged with her.

I heard the door of our crate open a few times, but since I could smell that Lacey was nowhere near, I did not even bother to get up as Dad reached in to pick up one of my siblings. What did it matter what happened now? Lacey was gone!

After a while, Mother Dog yawned and rolled a little way away from me. I immediately missed the comforting press of her fur against me. I looked around to see that there were only three dogs in the crate now—Mother Dog, White-Face Sister, and me. My brothers and sisters had been removed from my life, just like Lacey.

Dad was standing outside the crate, and he opened it up and reached in and took White-Face Sister. He handed her to a tall, skinny man with some fur on his face, under his nose. The tall man laughed and hugged White-Face Sister. "Ready to go home, puppy?"

The man carried White-Face Sister away. If he had been the girl with long dark hair, I might have tried to be taken myself, taken to Lacey, but I could smell the tall man had not been anywhere near my best friend.

Mother Dog watched everything alertly, but she did not make a sound. Now it was just the two of us.

I realized I might never see Lacey again, and it made me whimper. My mother heard me and lowered her nose to me. Perhaps she knew why I was so upset. We both missed the other puppies (except maybe Heavy Boy), but I did not think Mother Dog understood how I felt about my Lacey.

In a little while, Dad opened the crate up again. He reached in and gently took hold of Mother Dog's collar.

"Come on, honey," he said to her gently. "Someone wants to meet you."

Mother Dog eased to her feet. She looked down at me once and then let Dad tug her out of the crate.

Dad closed the crate door behind her.

I was all alone now.

2

Mother Dog did not come back. Lacey did not come back. I was so upset and confused that I flopped down on the old towel in the crate where Mother Dog had been resting and breathed in her scent. I shredded a corner of the blanket, but that did not make me feel any better. I curled up in a ball, trying to comfort myself, but that did not work, either.

I didn't know what was happening, but I did not like it at all.

People kept walking back and forth outside the crate, and a few stopped to look at me. Some of them bent down to talk to me or put their fingers into the crate, but I did not even glance up at them. I could smell that they had not been with Lacey.

A few of those people talked to Dad or Ava. "Sorry,

no, that one's spoken for," Dad told them. Or Ava would say, "No, that's Cooper, and he's already got a family. We're just waiting for them." And the people would leave. I lay alone on the towel, missing Mother Dog. Missing Lacey. Even missing my littermates.

I noticed that Dad and Ava were carrying some empty crates back to the big truck we had all been in before. "Great event!" Dad told Ava.

"What about Cooper?" Ava asked. She sat down near my crate to peer in at me.

"I don't know what happened. They said they'd be here," Dad replied.

Ava leaned forward. "I'm so sorry, Cooper," she whispered to me. "I know you miss Lacey. And I'm sorry your family didn't come. But you'll have a good life, I promise."

I heard her say, "Lacey," and picked up my head to look around and sniff. But Lacey was not anywhere near. I flopped my head back down on my paws, wrapped up in my sad feelings, listening to the quiet as all the humans left except Ava and Dad, who finished loading all the crates.

After a while, I heard people approaching, but I didn't lift up my head to look at them. "So sorry we're late," a man's voice said. "We ran into some road construction."

Dad's voice answered, "That's okay. We were just finishing up."

The door to my crate opened. I glanced up as Dad reached in and wrapped his hands around me to pull me gently out.

There were three new people. One was a tall man. The other was a boy, older than Ava. And the third was a boy, too, smaller than the first boy but still bigger than Ava. He was sitting in a chair with wheels.

Dad set me on the lap of the boy in the chair.

I'd been in Ava's lap plenty of times, but I'd never sat in the lap of a boy before. He smelled very interesting! Clinging to his T-shirt was the faint odor of sweat, and there was a little stain on the front where something greasy had fallen. I licked that up for him. Then, naturally, I had to lick his face.

The boy was smiling down at me and laughed and pulled his face away when I licked it. I put my front paws on his chest and sniffed his hair and checked under his ears.

He laughed some more.

"Cooper, huh? Cooper, you're a good little dog," he told me. Humans always know a dog's name. I nibbled his fingers a little. He'd been holding something sweet recently. "You're going to be my service dog, Cooper. You'll help me do everything."

Dad made a confused noise. "You didn't tell me you

wanted Cooper to be a service dog," he said to the other man.

The man nodded. "It's Burke's idea," he said, putting his hand on the shoulder of the boy in the chair. The boy was holding me tightly. If he relaxed his grip, I realized, I might have the chance to jump down and see if I could find Lacey.

"But a dog like that needs a lot of training," Dad objected. "Specialized training. There are organizations that do that kind of thing. You should contact them. Cooper's just a puppy. He hasn't had any training at all, really."

"I know," the other man replied. "We've been on a waiting list to get a service dog for Burke, but that's going to take a long time."

"And I can't wait any longer," the boy declared. I stuck my face into the folds of his T-shirt to see if there was any more food to lick. "I'm starting sixth grade next fall, and I need a dog for that. So I'm going to train Cooper by myself."

"Middle school, eh? I guess I understand. But raising a puppy to be a service dog is a pretty big commitment," Dad observed, looking from the boy to the other man. "It's going to be a lot of work. A lot of *hard* work. And some dogs just don't have the temperament for it. They wind up being happier as pets."

The other man looked down at my boy with a quick smile. "Hear that, Burke? That's what Grandma and I have been telling you."

"And I keep telling you *I know*, Dad," the boy replied. "Whoever said I was scared of hard work?"

The other man laughed. Dad shook his head with a smile. "Well, sounds like you know what you're getting into," he said. "We want to place animals with families that take care of them, and if you're going to be spending that much time training Cooper, then, regardless of whether he becomes a service dog or not, I know he's in good hands."

My boy grinned. He put his hands on the wheels that were on either side of his chair, leaving me balanced by myself on his lap. I was preparing myself to leap down and dash off in the direction the black-haired girl had taken Lacey when he shoved the wheels.

The chair moved! I lurched and wobbled on his lap, and I lay down as quickly as I could.

The other boy, the taller one, had wandered off a little while we were talking. He was kicking at a stand of grass with his back to the rest of us.

"Come on, Grant!" the other man called. "Let's go!"

"Wait!" came a high voice. "I have to say goodbye to Cooper!"

Ava came running across the grass to us. She bent

down to me where I sat in the boy's lap and kissed my head and scratched my neck the way she did so well.

"Goodbye, Cooper," she whispered. "I hope I get to see you again. And I hope you see Lacey, too."

She seemed happy and sad at the same time. She kissed me again, and then the boy started to push his wheels some more, and the chair moved. We headed away while Ava and Dad waved to us.

I was leaving, leaving the way my littermates and my mother had left. The way Lacey had left. Where was I going?

It struck me that this fit the pattern of the day, with humans taking dogs, including Mother Dog and my littermates, and departing with them. I wagged excitedly. Clearly, I was being taken to rejoin my family and Lacey!

First, we took a long car ride in a different sort of truck from the one Ava and Dad drove—instead of being very large, with rows of dog crates stacked on big shelves, this one had seats and an open place in the back for the chair with wheels.

I sat in the lap of the smaller boy. I sniffed the bigger boy, and when the man in front turned around and reached a hand back to me, I sniffed that, too. I was beginning to understand that all three of these people were a family. They had a smell that connected them,

18

just as my littermates and my mother and I had a family smell of our own.

The truck started moving. The boy from the chair pressed a button on the door next to him. "Want to sniff out the window, Cooper?" he asked me.

I liked to have him say my name. He kissed me on my nose and held me to his chest. "You're such a good dog, Cooper," he told me. The way he said my name carried so much affection it made me wiggle.

It occurred to me then that this boy was different from anyone I'd ever met—not because he could roll his chair but because of the way he looked at me and spoke to me. Up until then, I'd been cuddled by Ava and petted by Dad, but I'd never felt such pure, focused love pouring from them. This boy, I realized, wanted to be my boy, the way Lacey was my dog.

I'd never before considered that I might someday have my own boy.

Then I noticed the entrancing smells rushing in through the open window, so I jumped up to put my front feet on the glass. I lifted my nose up as high as I could and sniffed and sniffed and sniffed, searching for Lacey.

The boy laughed and rubbed my back. He was nice.

The people talked and, after a time, I started to understand that the bigger boy was Grant and the smaller boy was Burke, the way I was Cooper and Lacey was Lacey.

I balanced on Burke's lap until I was too tired to sniff anymore. Then I collapsed and fell asleep as the truck hummed and rumbled around us.

I woke when it stopped moving. "Welcome home, Cooper," Burke told me. He held me while the man stepped out of the car and came around and opened the door.

The man took me and put me down on the ground. My bladder was full, so I squatted and took care of that. The man and Burke seemed very excited about that and said my name a lot. I didn't know what they were talking about, but they seemed happy that I had peed in the grass.

These people were easy to please.

Then I looked around. I was in a very big yard. I had never been loose in a yard so big before. I lifted my nose to sniff. I smelled so many things my mind reeled.

There were smells I recognized—grass, warm in the sun, and water somewhere nearby, lots of water. And I also smelled animals. Not dogs. Not squirrels. Not even cats—now and then, I'd met a cat at my old home.

Naturally, I wanted to follow my nose and explore these unknown animals. And I started to do just that, taking a few steps before a thought occurred to me. Being held in Burke's lap, whether in the truck or the rolling chair, gave me no chance to do what I had decided I must do, which was to set off in search of Lacey. Finding Lacey was even more important than sniffing out new animals, wasn't it?

I could choose right there, I realized, between my normal life with Lacey and a new life here in this strange place.

I picked Lacey. She couldn't be far—she had *never* been far! Surely, I needed only to follow the dirt road a little bit, or turn toward the fields, or make my way to the water, and her scent would come to me.

I headed away from the people, across a hard dirt road, and into some grass tall enough to brush my belly. No sign of Lacey yet.

"Grant!" the man called out. "Go catch the puppy!"

In a moment, Grant was running along with me. I decided this was fine. Perhaps he could help me. Humans were good at opening doors and things like that. We might find Lacey in Dad's big truck, and then Grant could open the door to let me in.

"Hey, Cooper, wait!" Grant shouted behind me. "Cooper, come!"

I heard Grant saying my name, though I had no idea why. He jogged up behind me and made a grab at my collar, but I dodged sideways. This was no time for collar-grabbing.

"Cooper, c'mon!" Grant said. I looked back to see that

he was now on his hands and knees in the grass. He lunged, his hand reaching out, and I scampered away. When we found Lacey, I would be more than willing to play with Grant, but not right now.

Without a glance backward, I took off.

3

I wasn't as fast as Lacey, but I could run. Soon I found myself at the top of a small hill, where grass rolled smoothly down to a giant puddle, the biggest I'd ever seen. There were animals floating on the surface of that puddle, animals who made odd quacking noises. Were they the kind of animals that you could chase? I plunged down the hill toward them, thinking a quick little chase of some floating quackers would be a good side trip before I went back to finding my Lacey.

"Don't go in the pond!" Grant yelled from behind me.

He came galloping down the hill after me, which made everything even more exciting. The two of us would jump in the water, catch a few of the animals, and then continue looking for Lacey. But then Grant surprised me by snagging my collar. "You're not going anywhere, Cooper!" He scooped me up with one hand under my belly.

I squirmed and wiggled, but he didn't set me down. Instead, he carried me away from the grass and all the animal smells and into a building that smelled like the people from the truck. Grant held me above the floor as we entered a room that I later learned was called the kitchen.

The kitchen was amazing. It did not smell of animals but of something even better—delicious food! My boy and the man were there, and there was a woman standing near a stove, stirring a pot that smelled so wonderful I started to drool. The floor smelled good, too. I wedged my nose into the space beneath the cupboards because there were some crumbs there, and it was important to take care of them right away.

The woman laughed. "That's the puppy? That's Cooper? Goodness, he's going to be as big as a horse! His feet are the size of baseball mitts!"

I liked the woman's laughing. I went to inspect her ankles.

"Good boy. Good Cooper!" she told me. I wagged up at her. I still did not understand where my family was or where Lacey had gone or what I was doing here, but I liked the smells of the kitchen. In a few minutes, I liked it even more, because Burke wheeled himself to a cupboard and pulled out a bag that smelled marvelous. He filled up a bowl with the stuff from the bag. Then he set the bowl on the ground.

Food for me! And even better, in my own bowl that I did not have to share with any brothers and sisters! I gobbled my dinner up. It felt so wonderful to have a full belly.

This kitchen was a good place. This farm was a good place. But even with my belly heavy with dinner, I still felt a strange sort of hunger inside when I thought of Lacey.

The people all talked while Burke and Grant put some clinking things on the table. The boys said the word *Dad* to the man a lot. Why were they talking about Dad and not Ava? Maybe this man was also Dad? But how was something like that even possible?

The woman's name, I decided, was Grandma. She kept stirring stuff on the stove and opening and closing the oven. Every time that oven door was pulled open, hot, delicious smells poured into the room.

Meat! I was pretty sure I wanted to climb into that oven, but then Grandma pulled the meat out and set it on the counter, so I wanted to climb up there instead. I put my paws up on a cupboard as far as I could reach.

Grandma pushed me down. "No, Cooper. No chicken for you."

I sat down at her feet and gave her my best imploring look, with my head cocked a little to one side and my ears dropping. It was a look that always caused Ava to give me a treat.

But it did not work at all with Grandma. She just laughed and carried plates full of that wonderful meat to the table.

"Should we put the puppy outside?" she asked. "We don't want him to get used to begging at the dinner table."

"No, we've got to start socializing him right away," Burke said. "That's what I read. He's got to get used to all kinds of situations and people. If we put him out, he won't learn how to behave."

"Well, you're the expert, I guess," Grandma said. The people all sat down at the table, and I padded over to be by Burke. I was sure he'd share his chicken with me—he seemed to like me more than anyone else. I put my paws on his legs.

Burke scooted me under the table. "Down there, Cooper. You stay there."

His hands smelled delicious. I licked at them eagerly. Then I sat and looked at all the feet. Two pairs in sneakers—they were Burke and Grant. One pair in boots had thick soles with lots of cracks—that was New Dad.

One pair in slim dark shoes with a buckle on the sides—
and that was Grandma. But no food for me.

I pawed a little at New Dad's boot. He shook me off.
I whined up at Grandma.

"Don't do anything," Burke advised. "Just ignore him."

I certainly appreciated the bowl of food I'd been fed
earlier, but this so-called chicken changed everything.
My nose filled with it so that I couldn't smell or think
of anything else. How could everyone be eating chicken
without giving me any?

But then Burke figured it out. His hand fell to his
lap, and a tiny bit of chicken dropped from his fingers
to the floor.

I pounced on it, chewing quickly.

Then Grant did the same thing, except he let a tiny
piece of bread fall. This was such an excellent development! I found a place to lie down right between Grant
and Burke and waited as patiently as I could for the
small pieces of food that now and then fell down.

"Cooper's quieted down so nicely," Grandma said. "I
guess you had the right idea, Burke, not paying any attention to him at the table. Do you really think you'll be
able to train him in time?"

"I have a whole year," Burke replied.

"Well, I know it seems like a long time to you boys,
but sixth grade will be here before you know it."

"We'll be ready," Burke said. "We can start service

dog training when Cooper's six months old, and until then, I can get started with basic dog commands like *sit*."

"I'm remembering what we heard at the adoption fair, that it isn't easy to train a service animal. We'll just have to see how it goes," New Dad said. "We could always do another year of homeschooling, and you and Cooper can start in seventh. If Grandma doesn't mind, that is."

"It's not that I mind," Grandma said. "But the math is getting to be a little much for me."

Burke made an exasperated kind of noise. "No, Dad. I want to start in *sixth grade*. That way middle school is new for everybody, all the students. I'm already going to be different because I'm the only one in a wheelchair. If I wait until seventh, I'll be the new kid on top of everything else. It would be an epic nightmare."

Grant made a snorting sort of noise.

"What's that supposed to mean?" Burke demanded.

"You must have pretty tame nightmares, if you call that epic," Grant said scornfully.

"It doesn't matter what the dream is if I wake up and see you in the other bed and realize you're my brother," Burke shot back. "That's the most epic nightmare of all."

"Boys," New Dad said.

The talking stopped.

After the people were done eating, they stood up. Grant carried plates over to the counter, where Burke was waiting in his chair by the sink.

29

Nobody seemed likely to drop any more pieces of chicken for me, so I trotted over to a corner and sniffed, looking for just the right spot. I found it and turned around a few times.

"Grant! Take Cooper out!" Burke exclaimed suddenly.

Grant came running over and snatched me up before I'd even started what I was about to do. He ran with me in his hands and banged through the screen door and plopped me down in the grass.

"Whoa! Just in time!" he panted.

Somewhat disgusted to have been interrupted, I squatted and finished doing what I'd started, leaving a pile of poop on the ground.

"Good dog, Cooper," Grant praised.

He patted me and rubbed my chest. That part was nice, but he could have patted me and rubbed me in the kitchen where the chicken was.

Grant and I headed back inside, and I padded into the kitchen, where Grandma and New Dad were banging plates and talking.

"I do think Burke's right," Grandma said as she wiped a plate with a towel. I watched carefully for falling chicken. "Being the new kid would be difficult after everyone has gotten to know each other in sixth grade, all the fifth graders transferring in from other schools, especially since he'll already be drawing attention."

New Dad grunted. "Seems like having a dog's going to attract a lot of attention, if that's the problem. He's a stubborn one, our Burke."

A little while later, Burke took me down a hallway to a room with three soft beds in it. Two of the beds were big and rectangular and high up off the ground, and one was small and round and lying right on the carpet.

Burke wheeled right over to that one. He bent down and patted it. "Here, Cooper. Here's your bed," he told me. "Bed, Cooper. Bed."

I liked him saying my name and bending down low enough so that I could lick his face. Then I flopped down into the soft bed. It was very comfortable, and I was so tired.

I dozed and woke and dozed again as Grant and Burke did some odd things—taking off their clothes, throwing them at a basket in the corner, where several items landed on the floor. (I drowsily thought that maybe this was so I could get them out and chew on them later.) Then Burke maneuvered his wheelchair next to one of the big beds, pulled back the covers, and used his arms to hoist himself in. Grant touched a switch on the wall by the door, and the room suddenly went dark. He came over and slid into the other bed.

The room was quiet and peaceful.

Too quiet. Too peaceful.

I was lonely.

At night, I had always slept in a pile with my brothers and sisters and Mother Dog. When I napped during the day, it was often with Lacey, her chin on my back or my head burrowed into her soft stomach. My new bed was soft, but it felt chilly and empty. I wanted another warm body right next to mine.

I whined a little.

Nothing happened.

I whined louder.

"Cooper, be quiet," Grant groaned from his bed. "I'm trying to sleep."

I whimpered.

"Come on, Burke, how am I supposed to get to sleep with all that noise?" Grant said.

"He's keeping me awake, too," Burke said. "He's probably never slept alone before."

"Well, he's your dog. Do something."

There was a silence. I let out a long, heavy sigh through my nose. I missed Mother Dog. I missed Lacey.

The covers on Burke's bed rustled. There was a soft, dragging noise. Then I heard Burke's body drop into his chair.

"What're you doing?" Grant asked.

"Getting Cooper to be quiet because my brother's a big baby."

The wheels on Burke's chair squeaked. He rolled over to my bed and reached down to pet me.

I licked at his hand. Some of the lonely feeling dropped away.

Burke scooped me up and put me in his lap. Then he took both of us back to his bed. He put me in the middle of his covers, and then he pulled himself back into bed next to me.

"Better not let Dad or Grandma find out," Grant warned.

"I'm not going to tell them. Are you?" Burke asked.

"We'll just have to see if I do or I don't," Grant answered.

"You tell them I had a dog in my bed and I'll say you always sleep with the goat in yours," Burke advised.

Grant laughed. Then Burke laughed.

"Settle down, boys," New Dad called from somewhere deeper in the house.

I burrowed into the covers, making myself a warm nest close up against Burke's side. He put his arm around me. We both let out a long sigh.

I thought about my day and all the new smells and these people, who were very nice. But I didn't belong here. I was a dog who lived with other dogs, especially Lacey. A mistake had been made, bringing me to this place.

I would sleep now, but tomorrow I would leave here and return home. If Burke or Grant wanted to come with me, that was fine, but I couldn't stay here any longer, especially if everyone was going to be getting big pieces of chicken except me.

Lacey was waiting for me, I was sure of it. She and Ava were probably wondering where I was right now.

The thought made me sad.

4

Burke and I slept together all night long. In the morning, I stood up and stretched and shook until the tags on my collar jangled. Burke opened his eyes and groaned.

"Cooper, it's only five thirty," he told me.

I was glad to see him, too. I would go and lick his face in a moment. But first, I had something to do.

Burke sat up in bed as I scratched at the covers and squatted. Then he did something I did not expect at all—he pushed me right over the edge of the bed!

I landed paws-first on the carpet and shook my head indignantly. Why would a boy do something like that?

"Grant! Take Cooper out!" Burke shouted.

Grant groaned and kicked at his covers and sort of rolled out of bed. I was still getting my bearings when he scooped me up and ran with me, out of the room and down the hall and out the door and into the grass, just like last time.

It was such a relief when he set me down and I could pee!

"Good, Cooper, good boy!" Grant told me when I'd finished. He pulled something out of a pocket in his pajamas—a treat!

"I'm the fun boy in the family," Grant told me as I took the treat from his fingers. "Burke says you're a working dog, but when you're a little older, we'll go on hikes and I'll throw the ball for you. You'll see. With me, you get to be a regular dog. With Burke, he's going to do all this training so you can help him go to middle school."

The treat was delicious.

I looked around. I saw a big building, big as the house, just off to the side, and a long dirt path down to the pond. That would be the direction to go, past the pond and out into the world. I confidently headed out and hadn't gone more than two steps when Grant scooped me up off the ground.

"Where do you think you're going, you silly puppy?"

We went back inside to the kitchen, and for a second time, I was able to lie between Grant and Burke while the people ate at the table. "I'm going to start working on socializing Cooper right away," Burke said while he ate a piece of toast.

I liked toast. Very much. I wondered if Burke knew this about me.

"Tell me about socialization," Grandma said.

"Without it, dogs can become unpredictable in social situations. Like Grant."

Grant snorted.

"Puppies learn the world they're shown," Burke continued. "As a service dog, he needs to be comfortable in the world, to ignore distraction, and to be okay with other animals, children, and adults. I mean, think about it—we're going to be in middle school. I can't depend on every kid and teacher to know not to interfere with Cooper while he's working. He's going to have to get used to chaos. I'm going to expose him to as many different experiences as I can."

"How are you going to do that? He's not even house-trained yet. You can't take him anywhere," Grant objected.

"Yeah, but people can come *here*," Burke explained. "It's so important, we're starting today."

Whatever they were discussing, it did not lead to toast. Instead, Burke clipped something called a *leash* into my collar. Then he sat and watched while I twisted at the end of it, unable to move very far without being pulled up short. "You have to learn there's no escaping the leash, Cooper," he told me.

I did not like the leash thing, especially when Burke rolled down the ramp to the yard and I was dragged along behind him. How could I find my way back home when I was tied to his wrist?

I watched curiously as Burke lowered himself to the grass, hoisting his legs with his arms. It was a struggle and took some time, but finally, he was down at my level. "Cooper! Sit!" he told me, raising a finger in the air with one hand and pushing down on my rump with another.

None of this made any sense to me. "Sit!" He pushed more forcefully. What were we doing? I turned away and stretched to the end of the leash, thinking longingly of my plan to return to Lacey and Ava and Mother Dog. That was my purpose, not to be spoken to and pushed around by this toast-hoarding boy, who responded to my actions by pulling me back to him.

"Sit!"

He gently pressed my butt to the ground, and then he did something I did appreciate, which was to hand me a treat. I chewed thoughtfully. Clearly, if I pulled at the end of my leash, I would be rewarded.

After a long, long time of his irritating "Sit!" commands, his hand pushing on my rump, I finally made a connection. When he raised his finger and barked out that word, all I had to do was place my butt in the grass, shove or no shove, and I'd be fed a treat.

It seemed like a lot of bother, but those treats made it all worthwhile.

We were still playing Sit when a big truck bounded up the dirt driveway. I could scarcely believe my nose when the doors popped open. It was Ava! And Dad! (Old Dad, not the New Dad who lived here on the Farm.) And a new small person that Old Dad was carrying in his arms!

Ava had come to take me home, take me back to my littermates and to Lacey. I would not have to make my way on my own.

"Cooper!" Ava called as I twisted and pulled at the end of the leash. I whimpered and licked her hands when she bent down to me. She swept her light-colored hair away from her eyes and smiled at Burke. "Hi," she greeted shyly.

"Hi. Thanks for doing this," Burke replied.

Grandma came outside to make peeping noises at the small human in Old Dad's arms, while Burke told me "Sit!" in a stern voice.

Sit. At a time like this, with so much going on. I would not miss this place when I left with Ava and Old Dad.

But when I did Sit, Ava clapped her hands and said, "Good dog, Cooper." Burke handed me a treat, so I decided I could tolerate Burke's commands for now.

Grandma helped Burke into his chair. I watched curiously as Old Dad handed down the small human. "This is Billy," he said.

Burke held the child the way he had held me in the car. I sniffed at it curiously.

"Cooper seems fine with him," Old Dad observed. "I didn't really worry—puppies and toddlers nearly always get along. Why don't you put him down on the ground, Burke?"

"Are you sure?" Grandma asked a bit worriedly.

"Just hold the leash, Burke," Old Dad replied.

Burke lowered the child to the ground.

I had never seen a person this small before, and I'd never seen one who walked the way he did, wobbling with every step. He seemed about to fall over! The new person—Billy?—smelled very young and a little like milk and a little like pee, too. When he sat down, he reached out with both hands and grabbed my fur and pulled himself back up. As the baby did so, Old Dad held my head in his hands and smiled down at me. "Good, gentle dog," Old Dad told me.

"Good dog, Cooper," Ava praised.

Later, we played a game where I had a ball and Ava and Billy chased me around. Billy was unable to keep up and kept sitting down. I got tired and looked forward to napping in the car.

"Better get going," Old Dad remarked.

"Thanks for bringing Billy over," Burke told Ava and Old Dad.

"Glad to do it," Old Dad told him. "You're getting a great start on socializing Cooper, and we love to see that with the animals we adopt out."

"I'll come visit Cooper anytime," Ava added happily. She smiled at Burke and me both. "I can bring friends and other dogs."

"I'll take you up on that," Burke said.

I wagged when Old Dad swung Billy up off the ground, and when Ava and I followed them both to their truck, I was happy that Burke was coming with us, keeping pace so that the leash didn't tug at my collar. I was beginning to grow fond of the boy—he had kept me warm in bed and had been very generous with treats during his odd Sit phase. I knew Lacey would like him.

But then Ava and Old Dad got into their truck and I didn't. I pulled at the leash, not understanding, and whimpered when they drove away.

Weren't they taking me back home with them?

Burke liked the leash so much, he snicked it into my collar whenever he took me outside. I hated it. I was able to explore the Farm only at the end of it and had no opportunity at all to find my way home because of it.

We didn't go very many places, but we still met a lot of people. They came over in cars and on bicycles, and sometimes there were little children and sometimes they were older. The days were warm and sunny.

I learned to go to the door when I wanted to pee, and someone, usually Grant, would let me outside. Even he used the leash! Once we were back indoors, Grant would hurry to get dressed and say the word *school* a lot, and then he would go for a car ride. New Dad would do something similar, although he said *work* instead of *school*.

After they were gone, Grandma and Burke would sit at the kitchen table. "Let's start with your French lessons," Grandma would say, and Burke would groan.

Did they really think this was my purpose, to lie around while Grandma and Burke talked and talked? Did they not understand I had a dog family to sleep with and Lacey to wrestle with?

I would roll on my back or jump on a toy or run around the room to make sure they knew there were plenty of fun things to do. They didn't have to sit at that table and stare at a flickering box that didn't even smell tasty, or tap with their fingers on something that clicked, and just generally ignore the fact that they had a dog in the house.

Only after what seemed like forever did we have any fun at all. People would arrive around the time Grant came home—Grant's friends, I concluded, because they were boys and girls his age. Old Dad dropped off Ava and friends her age sometimes as well. All of them wanted to play with me, and after a long afternoon of flickering and clicking and sighing and talking, I was so happy to oblige them. I was passed around and kissed and snuggled and wrestled with, until I went from being so bored I could barely keep my eyes open to being so tired I could barely keep my eyes open.

"How's the socialization going?" Grant asked Burke.

"Really excellent," Burke enthused. "You can tell Cooper thinks of himself as a people dog now. Thanks for bringing over everybody."

"Oh, listen, I'm like most popular for having a puppy," Grant boasted. "Every girl in sixth grade wants to come over to visit Cooper. And, of course, Ava likes to come over to visit *you*."

"What?"

Grant just laughed.

"Ava's like in fourth grade," Burke said hotly.

"And you're a big fifth grader, I get it."

"She's helping with my dog. That's all," Burke insisted.

"You must really like her if you're this riled up by a few innocent comments," Grant observed. "Speaking of, when's Wenling coming back to town? She hasn't been in school."

"I think today. She's been helping her dad."

"Ava's going to be jealous, she catches you hanging out with Wenling," Grant said with a smirk.

Burke groaned and wheeled out of the room, and I had to follow, of course, because I was on the leash. I didn't understand the purpose of the leash indoors, where there was no chance of me getting away, but Burke loved the thing so much he often left it on me.

Burke and I wrestled together on his bed for a while, and then he clutched me to his chest. "I love you, Cooper," he whispered.

There was such affection in the way he held me I just had to lick his face.

And then I realized something.

Burke wasn't just a boy to me anymore. He was *my* boy. There was no denying it. I loved everyone in the Farm family, but I loved Burke most of all, and I could feel that he loved me, too.

Which put me in an odd situation. I knew where I belonged, and it wasn't here. I knew with whom I belonged, which was Lacey and my dog family. But could I leave Burke?

No, I realized. I could not.

When I left to go home, Burke would have to come with me.

The next day, Burke took me out into the yard to play Come, which was where he would say, "Come," and then haul on the leash until I was right at his side, and then he'd give me a treat. It was a little like Sit, only with movement. Eventually, I learned that when he said, "Come!" it was just easier to trot back to him than to wait for him to drag me across the grass. Once I did that, though, there were no more treats for him pulling me to his side with the leash. I had to do Come on my own for a morsel.

Grant came home, so I thought it likely I would soon see Ava or some other people to play with.

Then Burke dropped the leash. I stared at it—I had not been free for a long, long time. He backed his chair away from me until there was some distance between us.

I turned and looked down the driveway. This was the chance I had been waiting for. But would my boy follow me? And if he didn't, what then?

I missed my family, and I missed Lacey. Since arriving on the Farm, I had wanted nothing more than to leave, to go home. Did having my own boy change that?

"Cooper! Come!" Burke called.

I gazed at him. He clapped his hands. "Come!" he said again. "Come! Cooper, Come!"

5

I did Come back to my boy, and he gave me a treat. It was as simple as that. I had always thought of myself as a dog who lived with many other dogs, a dog who loved Lacey and who was fed by Ava and Old Dad. But now I was a dog with my own boy.

I no longer strained at the leash when Burke took me outside, but followed him willingly. We often journeyed down to the big body of water, which I learned was called the pond. Floating on the surface of the pond were the quacking birds called *ducks*. Burke would wheel out to the end of the ramp that jutted out into the water (the "dock") to the pond, where I would bark at the ducks, who didn't seem to understand how afraid they were supposed to be of a dog.

"Cooper! Sit!" Burke always said, interrupting my

barking. I immediately did Sit for the treat that followed. "How come you don't get this, you silly dog? You're not supposed to bark at the ducks when I'm with you. You need to ignore them. What, you think a service dog can run around barking?"

Other times, we would visit a strange animal who lived in a pen next to the barn. "This is Judy; she's an old goat," Burke informed me. She was much taller than I was, with shaggy fur and two horns on her head. I could see that she was chewing grass. Maybe she was going to throw up later. That's what happened to me when I ate grass.

"Hey, Cooper," Burke murmured. I looked at him, and he fed me a treat!

I loved my boy.

"You're doing exactly the right thing. You're not at all frazzled by a goat, and you turn away to me when I call. Good dog."

I liked being called good dog, and I liked being fed treats.

We were doing something new out in the yard— Stay, Burke called it, when a car ground its way up the dirt driveway. I could tell by the sound it made that it wasn't Ava and Old Dad.

I was glad to turn away from Stay, which was a really unpleasant game where I was supposed to do Sit for a long, long time without moving. I became especially alert when I heard a dog in the new car, yipping out the window.

I knew that yip.

I raised my head sharply, drawing air deeply into my nose. It was faint, but familiar and unmistakable. I knew that smell as well as I knew my own.

Lacey.

Lacey had come to find me! She soared out the open car window and hit the ground at a run. I felt Burke's hand on my collar, and he said, "Okay!" and then with a snick I was off leash and dashing up to greet my dog.

Lacey was as happy to see me as I was to see her. We jumped on each other and rolled in the grass. It was impossible to tell which of us was chasing the other or who was jumping and who was being jumped on. Lacey flopped on her back, and I dove on top of her and gnawed on her face and neck as gently as I could. My jaws quivered with happiness to be back with my best friend.

"Well, I guess they like each other," Lacey's girl said as she approached my boy's chair.

"Looks like it," Burke agreed. "Thanks for bringing her, Wenling. What's her name? Lacey?"

Lacey picked her head up when she heard her name and wagged. Then she wiggled out from under me and jumped back with her rump and tail high, asking me to play.

Of course I wanted to play!

Burke maneuvered his chair through the grass. The girl followed. Lacey and I joyfully tore around in wide circles. Lacey found a stick and grabbed it and shook it in her mouth, so of course I had to try to grab it, too. We spun around and around and then played Tug. The stick broke, and I wound up with the biggest piece, so I ran, and Lacey did Chase.

Burke and Lacey's girl followed us as best they could. We tore through the barn, which was a big, mostly empty room. Lacey was astonished by the horned animal in the pen next to it, and she stopped to bark, so I joined her, barking as well.

"Lacey! Cooper!" Lacey's girl shouted, running up to us. "Don't bother Judy." The girl grabbed hold of Lacey's collar and pulled her away.

"Come on, this way, Lacey. Let's go!" She ran a few steps, so of course we ran, too. Running with Lacey was wonderful.

We soon crested the top of the smooth hill that led down to the pond. Lacey and I galloped down the slope straight toward the water.

I was so happy to show Lacey the ducks! She and I leaped into the shallows and barked our loudest, and the ducks spread their wings and flapped hard and flew off, which was very satisfying. The ducks might ignore one dog, but obviously, two dogs terrified them.

We splashed out of the water and flopped down on the dock together. The sun felt so good on my fur. I chewed gently on Lacey's leg, and she put her paw on my head.

We lay there, panting, loving being together. Our boy and our girl came down to be with us. Burke's wheels made a crunching sound as they rolled over the gravel path and onto the dock.

"Well, I guess that went well," the girl observed.

"Yeah," Burke answered, coming to a stop. I wagged to see him. I loved Burke. I loved Lacey. I would be happy to love Lacey's girl, too. Now I understood why I'd had to leave my first home, with Ava and Old Dad and Mother Dog and my brothers and sisters. It was so I could come here to the Farm, to live with my boy and Lacey and teach those ducks to be afraid of dogs.

"I knew these two were at the shelter together," Burke went on. "I guess they were already friends. There was no hesitation in either one of them."

The girl flopped down next to us. I thought about chewing her leg, too, like I was chewing Lacey's, to show that I was fond of them both. But I only had one mouth, so I couldn't.

Lacey and I both alerted when the ducks, after flying in circles above us, landed with light splashes *right back in the pond*. Lacey and I stared at each other in shock,

unable to believe it. Hadn't we just shown those ducks we were to be feared?

"I guess I should bring Lacey whenever I come over," the girl said. "These two belong together."

"Yeah, it's been weird not to see you. How was your summer vacation?"

"Vacation!" the girl repeated. "I spent every day with my dad, helping build my uncle's house down in Indiana—even though mostly what I did was watch them work and bring them stuff. Dad wouldn't let me use any of the power tools. I learned to paint, though—it's not as easy as it looks." The girl stiffened slightly, and both Lacey and I glanced at her.

"It's okay," Burke said mildly. "I get that it would be even harder for me." He patted the wheelchair.

"I know you don't like to talk about it."

"No, it's okay. I don't mind anymore. It's like training Cooper has changed things."

"I mean, I kind of already know," the girl confessed. "My mom said it happened when you were born?"

"It was a complication at birth," Burke agreed. "I don't know much more than that, though I was there at the time."

The girl laughed. Lacey flopped down, and I put my head on her ribs. The ducks were lucky we were both tired, or we might have driven them from the pond forever.

"How is Cooper's training? I can't get Lacey to do anything," the girl said finally.

"Good and not good. He's learned Sit and Come, and we're working on Stay. His biggest problem is that sometimes he loses his focus. You saw them with the ducks. He's supposed to ignore all distractions," Burke replied.

"How do you teach him *that*?" the girl wondered. "Lacey barks at every car that goes by."

I glanced at Lacey to see if she knew they were talking about her. She did.

"Supposedly, you expose them to the distraction and then reward them when they ignore it. It's working about half the time. Which would be fine if Cooper were just a farm dog, but he's going to be a service dog, so he's got to learn," Burke replied.

Lacey looked at me to see if I understood they were talking about me. I did.

"He's a wonderful puppy, even if the service dog thing doesn't work out," the girl observed. Then she frowned. "What did I say? You have this look on your face."

"It's just that it *has* to work out," Burke replied. "I tried school in first grade, and it was *horrible*. All kids wanted to talk about was my chair. But when they see Cooper perform his service tasks, they'll want to talk about *him*. It will make all the difference."

It was wonderful to be lying in the sun with Lacey, near the people who had come into our lives. I heard

Burke calling her "Wenling," so I came to understand that was her name.

But after a while, something happened that was not so wonderful. A car drove up, and Wenling and Lacey jumped into that car and left—without me!

I stared up into Burke's face and whined, hoping he'd understand that this wasn't supposed to happen. Somehow, he had found Lacey, and now we all needed to be on the Farm together, staring at goats and barking at floating ducks. Humans could do anything. Why didn't Burke do *this*?

Burke rubbed my chest.

"Don't worry, Cooper. She'll come back," he told me. "You'll get to play with Lacey. Wenling's my best friend."

We went back to playing Stay. I surely did not like that one.

Many days went by, the days grew cooler, and often Wenling and Lacey would come to visit! Lacey and I would tear around and leap on each other, dashing everywhere, frightening ducks and playing with sticks.

It seemed like every time Wenling came to the door, she looked different. Sometimes she had something on her head—those were called hats. Some hats were big and floppy, and some were snug against her skull. But she was still Wenling, no matter what she wore.

Grant liked to do the same thing. He would come to the door wearing very odd things that he never wore inside the house—heavy jackets that covered up his whole body, or boots that clumped loudly, or scarves that he hung around his neck. Sometimes he carried long sticks that he leaned on. Once he had a stick that he pointed at my nose. It made a whooshing sound and puffed out into a big round ball! I stared at it, unsure how I was supposed to feel about it. But Grant put it on the ground, and it didn't move, so I eased up to sniff it cautiously.

"Cool, Grant, thanks," Burke said. "The umbrella was a good idea."

"Cooper seems pretty chill about all of it," Grant observed.

"That's the idea. If he's going to be my service dog, I need him to ignore anything out of the ordinary, like people in hats and even umbrellas opening right in his face," Burke replied.

"Wenling has a lot of great ideas for costumes. Tomorrow, she's fitting me with a cape," Grant said.

"A cape! What's your superpower?" Burke asked. "Burping?"

Other days, Ava would visit, sometimes with Old

Dad and sometimes with an adult who drove her and other children. Often, she brought other dogs, and I would be overjoyed, except Burke would call out, "Stay," and then I would have to sit there, embarrassed, while the visiting dog sniffed me up and down. It would take forever for Burke to say, "Okay!" so I could run and play.

One day, Ava brought a cat that scowled at me from inside a small crate. She set the crate down on the porch, near where my boy was sitting.

"This is Bartholomew. He's a cat who thinks he's a dog," Ava explained.

"What do you mean?" Burke asked.

"He's been playing with dogs since he was a kitten. He even eats with dogs." Ava opened up a door in the crate. The cat walked out and sat on the porch and stared at me.

"Cooper. Stay," Burke said softly.

Stay? With a cat right in front of me?

I had met cats back when I'd lived with Ava and Old Dad, but they'd always remained inside their crates. I'd never seen one come out before.

This one marched right up to me as I sat quivering, waiting for my boy to say Okay. Then he flopped on his back and reached toward me with his paws, just like Lacey would.

It was too much to expect that I could do Stay in the

presence of such a friendly cat. I lowered my muzzle and he gripped it, and we immediately began wrestling.

"Cooper," Burke sighed.

What a wonderful cat! When he bolted off the porch, I pursued eagerly, and when he turned to chase me, I dashed away.

"Come!" Burke called.

I was too excited, playing with my new friend, to do Come. I was a dog who played with other dogs and now with cats. It was my purpose to be a fun, happy dog.

I was sure my boy would understand.

6

But Burke did *not* understand. "Cooper!" he shouted sternly.

Something in his voice made me feel like a bad dog. I lowered my ears and trotted back to my boy.

"Sit! Stay!"

That again. I did Sit, while the cat, puzzled, ran up to me to continue our play.

"Cooper," Burke warned.

I whined in frustration, but I did Stay, while the cat wove in and out between my legs and batted playfully at my snout. Stay was like being attached to a leash, and Okay was like taking the leash off.

"He's being really good," Ava said.

"*Now* he is. But picture we're out somewhere and I really need him, and he suddenly runs off to chase a cat or a squirrel," Burke replied. "He broke Stay as soon as Bartholomew was out of the cage."

"Maybe you're expecting too much. He's still a puppy," Ava observed. She picked up the cat and put him back in the crate, from where he stared at me accusingly.

"What do you think Cooper'll do when he sees the horse?" Ava asked Burke.

"That's going to be interesting," Burke replied.

Ava petted me affectionately. "I'm in fourth grade," she announced to Burke.

"Yeah, I know," Burke told her. "I remember. I'm in fifth."

"Some of the other kids in my class have boyfriends or girlfriends," Ava said. "But I think that's dumb."

"Sure," Burke agreed cheerfully. "Definitely dumb."

"I'm not going to have a boyfriend until I'm old," Ava said, watching Burke carefully. "Like fourteen or fifteen."

Burke laughed a little. "Good idea."

"And then it'll be you," Ava said.

"I was thinking maybe you've got other animals? Like chickens—huh, what? What did you just say?"

I glanced at Burke curiously—he suddenly seemed tense.

"You're going to be my boyfriend when I'm old enough," Ava explained calmly. She beamed a big smile at Burke.

I heard Grant laughing from behind us on the other side of the screen door.

Ava started to run. "C'mon, Cooper, chase me!" she called.

Grant kept laughing. Burke turned toward the screen door. "Shut up, Grant!"

I watched tensely as Ava kept running. "Okay, Cooper!" Burke said, so I jumped up and ran after her.

I was glad we were all having so much fun together.

Now that Lacey kept coming over, life at the Farm was simply wonderful. Every now and then, I missed Mother Dog, or I thought of my littermates and wondered what had become of them. I hoped they had gone to Farms of their own and all had boys as wonderful as Burke. But I could never be sad or miss them when Lacey came over to play, which happened most days.

The trees had finished shaking down all their leaves, and the days turned colder, really cold, especially in the mornings when I went out to mark my territory. Then one morning, when Grant opened the door for me, the ground outside had changed. It was white! I stared at it in astonishment, and Grant laughed.

"Snow, Cooper. Snow!" he told me. "Go on, get out there!"

I wanted to stand at the open door and sniff the cold, wet smell for a little bit, but Grant put his foot under my tail and gave me a little shove, and before I knew it, I was standing in the stuff that was all over the ground.

I loved it. It smelled like water. Like cold, cold water. I rolled in it and jumped in it and buried my snout in it. Was it called *snow*? Was that why Grant kept saying that word?

When I peed in the snow, my pee made a steaming yellow puddle and sank. That was truly amazing! Snow was fun!

It was good that I liked it, because it turned out that there was going to be a lot of it. Many, many days when Grant opened the door for me in the morning, there would be piles of the stuff on the ground, and I could run in it and pee in it and come back in, panting and damp. New Dad hung a towel by the kitchen door, and Burke or Grant would rub me down when I came in.

"You're getting to be a big dog now, Cooper," Burke told me, hooking some belts around my chest. "Time for your harness."

A harness was a sort of a complicated collar, and from that day forward I always wore one or both.

One snowy day, New Dad and Burke and Grant and Grandma all went on a car ride and did not include me, which made me sad. When they came back, they brought a tree right into the house! I had always thought that trees were *outside* and chairs and tables and rugs and beds were *inside,* but the people set the thing upright in a corner of the living room while I sniffed it. It smelled sharp and tangy and wild, definitely an outside thing. What were the people doing, bringing it in here?

There just were a lot of human behaviors that a dog couldn't hope to understand.

Well, they all seemed so happy with having a tree in the house, I decided the best thing for me to do was lift my leg on it, but everybody shouted and startled me so much that I stopped what I was doing. Then Grant rushed me to the kitchen door and pushed me outside, which I thought was very strange.

I found a tree outside, where trees belong, and peed on it. There. Everyone else might be going a little crazy, but not me.

The family put a bunch of boxes under the tree, and one day, when both boys smelled very excited, they sat around and pulled paper off the boxes and opened them. They put one box in front of me, and I looked at it and then at Burke. What did he want me to do with it?

"It's for you, Cooper!" Burke told me. "Open it!" He rattled the big bow on top of the box. I eyed it suspiciously.

Burke ripped a little paper off the box. I knew about

ripping, and I liked doing it. He waggled the ripped paper in my face, and I took hold of it with my front teeth and pulled. It gave way with a very satisfying sound, so I pulled off the rest of the paper, and then Burke opened the box for me.

"Look, Ava sent you some homemade dog biscuits!" he told me. "And . . . um . . . something for me, too, I guess."

There was a plastic bag in the box that smelled very good, like peanut butter. Peanut butter is one of my favorite things. I nudged the bag with my nose until Burke took out a biscuit and gave it to me.

"Go on, Burke, open your present from Ava!" Grant prodded, grinning.

Burke gave Grant a sour look. "I'm sorry that Santa forgot again this year to bring you a new personality."

My boy pulled something else out of the bag. It was a long strip of cloth. Perfect for tugging! I jumped at it, but Burke pulled it away from me.

"It's a scarf," he said. "Um. She made me a scarf, I guess."

Grant fell over laughing. "A pink scarf!"

Burke threw the empty box at Grant's head, and Grandma told Grant to sit up and behave like a human being, and New Dad chuckled.

After several days had gone by, the people took all the shiny stuff off the tree and dragged it back outside.

Apparently, that foolishness was over, though the smell of that tree lingered for a long time.

"Hey, I have great news," Grant announced while the family sat at the table and nobody was feeding a good dog fish.

"You're being adopted by a new family?" Burke guessed.

"Oh, Burke," Grandma said.

"You're finally going to get a brain transplant?" Burke guessed again.

"Let him talk, Burke," New Dad said.

"I made the soccer team! Practice is indoors until the weather clears," Grant said.

"That's great news," Grandma said. "Congratulations."

"Good job, son," New Dad said.

"I thought you were playing basketball still," Burke objected.

Grant's hand came down, but there was nothing in it for me to eat. He scratched his leg.

"Yeah, intramural basketball, just at the school. League basketball is over," Grant explained.

"What's the matter, Burke? Why that look?"

Burke pushed away from the table. "May I be excused?"

"Burke," New Dad said gruffly. "Explain yourself."

I nosed Burke's hand. He seemed a little sad.

"Just . . . I go to all Grant's games. And I cheer and I

sit there wondering about what it would be like to play a sport. Be part of a team," Burke responded.

Everyone was quiet a moment.

"Well, hey . . . ," Grant started to say, but Burke wheeled his chair to his room, and I followed.

When the piles of snow outside had started to melt and the ground was slushy and muddy and wet, Burke and I stayed inside, learning new things, like Lie Down. Which wasn't to say we didn't play. In fact, we spent most of the time playing. I had a lot of toys in a box in the living room—toys to throw, to squeak, or to tug on.

The only toy I never really liked was one Grant had gotten for me. "It's a nylon bone for him to chew; it's good for his teeth," Grant told Burke. He would thrust this odorless, tasteless thing in my face and shake it. "Get the bone! Want the bone?" he'd ask. I had to pretend to be interested in it because I felt sorry for him. Poor Grant, he couldn't find a fun toy out of a whole box of them.

A new toy usually was announced with a crinkle of stiff wrapping material, so I was very alert when Burke brought one out. Burke showed it to me. I sniffed eagerly, then felt my enthusiasm going away. This new toy seemed about as much fun as the nylon bone. It was a small metal thing with a button on it, and it smelled very boring. Burke pressed the button, and it made a click. That was really all it did. I looked at him questioningly.

Burke pulled out a bag of treats, and I immediately became much more interested. "Ready for the clicker, Cooper?" he asked. He clicked the thing, and he tossed me a treat.

Well, now that I understood the circumstances, I decided I liked the clicker! Each time it made its distinctive noise, I was given a small treat—no, not just small, tiny. But with enough clicks, the treats added up to an afternoon of deliciousness.

When Burke turned away from me and pulled out a phone and tapped it, I wandered around the living room. Sometimes when New Dad sat in a big chair, he dropped small pieces of food on the floor. But the moment Burke clicked, I returned eagerly to his side without him having to say anything, and I was rewarded with yet another treat! This was certainly more fun than chewing on a bone that didn't taste like anything.

After that, Burke was never without the clicker, and the treats just kept coming.

"Focus!" Burke told me one day in the voice he used when he was commanding me.

That was an odd one. After he said the word, Burke just sat there. I sat next to him. I wondered if there was something he wanted me to do. I tried doing Lie Down, which is often very popular. But it didn't seem to work this time. No clicks, no treats.

I looked up at Burke's face to see why we weren't doing anything interesting, and the clicker went *click*! Burke tossed me a treat.

Things were improving!

Then Burke said that strange word again. "Focus!"

I scratched my ear. No click-and-a-treat for that. I yawned. Now what? I looked at Burke.

Click! Treat!

Click meant *treat*. *Focus* meant . . . I didn't know what it meant, but it seemed that sometimes it meant *click,* and sometimes it didn't. I looked at Burke for guidance.

Click! Treat!

After we tried it several more times, I figured out that "Focus!" meant looking right at my boy and getting a treat for it. It didn't make much sense, but then "Stay!" doesn't make any sense either, and people seem to like that one a lot.

After a few days, Burke started to forget to do the click right away, and I would have to stare very hard for a long time to remind him. At last, if I kept staring, Burke would say, "Okay!" and there would be a click and a treat. There was much I didn't understand, but I did know I was doing what my boy needed.

When Wenling brought Lacey over, we'd race and wrestle and play-growl and love each other, and then we'd return back to our people and love them, too.

"Cooper needs a break from training, so thanks for bringing Lacey," he said to Wenling.

"Oh, Lacey loves Cooper. I swear that's all she ever thinks about."

I loved Lacey and Wenling. I loved New Dad and Grandma and Grant and Ava and Old Dad. But Burke was my boy. I loved Burke the most, because I had a sense that he *needed* me in a way the others didn't. Fulfilling that need was my purpose.

"You've done such a good job with Cooper. I've got Lacey doing sit and come here, but only when she feels like it," Wenling said.

"Well, Cooper's good at performing commands, but tomorrow I'm going to test him in real-life situations," Burke replied. "It's time to get serious. Cooper needs to learn to work."

7

The next day, Grandma drove Burke and me on a car ride to a park where children, many smaller than Ava, were running around and climbing on things and swinging and making a lot of noise. They were having so much fun I couldn't help but wag furiously.

"You have to stay with me, Cooper," Burke murmured quietly.

I heard him say my name. *Yes!* I wanted to go play with the children.

"No, Cooper," he murmured.

There was nothing "no" about all these children. I whined, eager to burst out of the door and go jump on them and play with them. Then I saw a small white dog race into the middle of everything, wagging and jumping. Now I could play with a little dog, too!

"Not good that he's crying," Burke observed.

"Can't you tell him to stop?" Grandma wanted to know.

"I shouldn't have to tell him to calm down. He's supposed to know that he's a service dog and that playing is only allowed when I say the release word."

Grandma brought Burke's chair around to the car door for him, and he swung himself into it, pushing on my chest to keep me in the car. When finally he said, "Come," I plunged out and ran to the end of the leash, wanting only to get to the park and have fun with the children and the dog.

"Oh *no!*" I heard Grandma cry.

I was straining as hard as I could but couldn't manage to move forward at all. I glanced back at my boy and was startled to see him sprawled on the sidewalk, his chair tipped over. Why did he do that?

"Cooper! Come!" he commanded sternly.

Grandma moved to Burke's side. "No, Grandma, I want him to understand," Burke told her. "Cooper! Come!"

Burke sounded so angry, and the children seemed so carefree, I was torn. What I wanted was to go play. What my boy wanted was for me to *not* play. What should I do?

With a last, frustrated glance at the children in the

park, I trotted to Burke and lowered my nose to him. What were we doing?

Click. Burke handed me a small treat, which I appreciated, but I felt that lying on the cement was a lot less fun than chasing children would be. I was as fun as the little white dog—why wouldn't Burke let me be the dog I was meant to be?

"Are you hurt, Burke?" Grandma asked.

Burke grunted as he sat up. "No, but that was a complete fail on his part. Really bad. Cooper, if you're going to help me, you have to learn to avoid distractions. And you can *never* drag me out of the chair!"

I was disappointed when we all loaded back into the car. This felt like going to a dog park to watch dogs instead of playing with them. As we pulled away, I gave a final, sad glance to the children scaling the equipment, the small white dog still running around at their feet.

Soon, we stopped by the side of the road, and Burke rolled the window partway down so I could put my head out and sniff.

"This is the busiest fire station in the county," Grandma noted.

"Thanks, Grandma. Hopefully, we won't have to wait too long."

"What's the point of this exercise?" she asked.

"Dogs have such good hearing that a really, really

loud noise can frighten them. I need Cooper to understand that no matter what is going on, he is supposed to
pay attention to me."

"Maybe wave a dog treat in front of his nose?"
Grandma suggested with a chuckle.

I glanced at her. *Treat? Dog?* I knew these words—
they were important words!

"That's exactly what I'm going to do. He'll be distracted from the sirens and eventually come to ignore
them—and hopefully all other noises. When it comes to
people, he's supposed to be distracted by *me*. Little kids
shouldn't matter."

There was a big building opposite us with giant
doors. One of those doors started to roll up, and Burke
grinned. "Yes! We lucked out!"

"Burke, if a fire engine is going out, there's an emer-
gency somewhere," Grandma pointed out. "Let's not describe it as 'lucky,' okay?"

Burke dug into his pocket as the biggest truck I had
ever seen rolled out through the giant door, vibrating so
loudly it rumbled my chest. It had a bright light on top
that flashed, and then suddenly, it made the most awful
sound—a loud, blasting shriek that turned higher and
louder.

I did not like it at all! But Burke was holding out a
treat for me, a soft, succulent morsel that I gobbled up
even as the wailing, flashing truck roared past. Burke

fed me more treats, and when I looked up from the last one, the truck was gone.

"Cooper, you're a brave, good dog," Burke told me. There were no more treats, but he was scratching behind my ears, which was almost as good. I leaned my head into his hand. "And tomorrow, we're going to go somewhere really exciting. Sort of like a combination of the playground, plus loud noises, plus a lot of other things."

"He did well with the fire engine," Grandma observed.

"He was awesome. But when it comes to people, he's such a playful love dog. He's way, way behind schedule. If I can't get him to understand, he won't be able to go to school in the fall."

We sat for a time in the car with the windows down so we could all smell for animals and other dogs. When the big doors starting rising and yet another gigantic truck trundled out, flashing and growling, I looked expectantly to my boy and was rewarded with another soft, meaty treat just as the air shattered with the high wail.

"Good dog, Cooper!" he praised.

People decide what behavior is good dog and what is bad dog, and it's not always obvious what the difference is, but I understood that when the screaming trucks blasted past us, I could get a treat, which seemed far more important than reacting to all the racket.

The next day, everybody seemed in a hurry in the morning, and Grant said, "School," and Burke and Grandma sat at the table, and Burke groaned. I followed my boy around to be sure he would not forget that dogs were important, even on busy days like this. In fact, in my opinion, we would be better off if we skipped all the groaning and went outside to bark at ducks.

"Happy Friday. Got to get to work," New Dad announced. He walked out the front door, but I remained at Burke's side because that's how these days went.

New Dad said, "Work," almost every day, but it was different from when Burke said it. I had learned that, to my boy, "Work" meant learning and practicing commands, and paying close attention to what he wanted from me. "Time to do some work, Cooper," Burke would say, and then we would do training in new commands or spend time doing old ones like Focus and Come and Sit.

While Grant and Burke were in their room getting dressed, Grant asked my boy something that made him go alert all over. I glanced curiously at both boys, feeling the odd tension in the room.

"Hey, Burke. I wanted to ask you something. So, Wenling. Is she, like, your girlfriend?"

Grant had his back to Burke and was digging around for something in a dresser drawer. Burke was pulling a shirt over his head. He struggled it down over his chest and stared at Grant.

"What? No way. I mean, we've been friends since like first grade. Girlfriend? No. It's like she's—I don't know—my cousin or something. I don't think about her like that . . . Wait a minute . . ."

Burke kept on staring at Grant. Grant kept on not turning around.

"Do *you* think of her like that? Like a girlfriend?" Burke asked.

Grant shrugged. "I don't know. I mean. She's kind of . . ."

Burke laughed a little. Grant spun around and glared at him. I sat by my boy's chair and looked back and forth from him to Grant. Was somebody angry here? Should I go and get a toy so we'd have something else to do?

"Don't laugh," Grant said sternly.

Burke's face turned serious. "I'm not laughing."

"Good."

"Okay, then."

"Fine. I have to get to school." Grant shut his dresser drawer and marched out of the room.

Burke laughed a little more. He leaned over me and rubbed my chest, and I licked his nose with affection.

"I think Grant likes Wenling, Cooper," my boy told me. "The way you like Lacey."

My ears went up. Lacey? Was Lacey here? I checked around, but she was not anywhere, so I snuggled my head into Burke's lap and loved him instead.

That evening, we took a long car ride, and everybody came—New Dad, Grandma, Burke, Grant. Not Lacey, though my boy said her name several times. I appreciated hearing her name but would appreciate seeing her even more.

"This is going to be really hard for Cooper," Burke murmured, stroking my head. I leaned into his hand a little. "Not just because of the kids but because of Lacey."

There, he'd said her name again.

"Not sure what you mean," New Dad said.

"It's because Lacey is Cooper's best dog friend," Grant explained. "Usually, when they see each other, they go nuts. But tonight, at the carnival, Burke's going to try to get Cooper to understand that it's not always playtime."

"Right," Burke agreed. "Sometimes, dogs just love each other. Happens to people, too. Even sixth graders like Grant."

Grant glared at my boy, who chuckled.

"In my day, we didn't call it a carnival; it was just the county fair," Grandma observed.

A little while later, the car stopped. "This is it, Cooper," Burke said. I lifted my nose. Lacey was here! Lacey and food and many, many people. As New Dad helped Burke into his chair, Lacey dragged Wenling over on her leash. We were all so happy!

"Let's give them some time to get used to this place," Burke suggested.

We took a walk, with Lacey and me getting our leashes tangled up and thumping gently into each other because we were so glad to be together. There were lots of people out taking walks, too, more than I'd ever seen. Some of them had food in their hands. Wonderful food! Hot dogs, ice cream, french fries! I wanted it all, and Lacey did, too. Her nose was twitching frantically.

This place was as big as a dog park, but it was filled with people and big, loud machines, some with flashing lights. One giant wheel soared high up into the air, and it spun around and around. People seemed to be sitting in little buckets on that wheel, and they waved and shouted. I'd never seen anything so strange, and I was a little nervous. We weren't going to be getting in one of those buckets, were we?

Other flashing, beeping, grinding machines twirled and lifted and flew, many full of screaming children. They weren't as loud as the big trucks from the day before, but they were a lot flashier. I decided to ignore them and perhaps a treat would be forthcoming.

Then Burke stopped his chair and called me to be with him while Grant and New Dad and Grandma walked away. "Stay, Cooper."

Sitting there was very hard to do, with so much going on. I wagged at all the smells and the people and the sounds. Lacey pulled Wenling toward some hot dog pieces scattered on the ground, and I wanted so badly to run with her and get those hot dogs that I quivered all over. Remaining with my boy was hard work. I climbed to my feet, practically tasting the treats Lacey was snatching up.

Burke stroked me and talked to me gently. "Steady, Cooper. I know it's tough, boy. Stay with me."

Wenling turned and waved, and she and Lacey vanished into the crowds! I sniffed furiously, finding and holding Lacey's scent. I glanced up at my boy. At any moment, I was ready to lunge out to the end of the leash and go have fun. Wasn't that the purpose of a dog, to play and play when people were laughing and tossing down hot dog bits and my favorite dog, my Lacey, had walked off with her girl?

What were we doing?

"Sit, Cooper."

I just couldn't do it, couldn't do Sit. I yawned anxiously. We needed to go find Lacey!

"School will have bells and kids and noise and fun, maybe not quite like this," Burke said in quiet tones, "but close enough. If you're going to go to classes with me, you have to be able to handle the hallways. You need to pay attention to me now, Cooper. Nothing else matters."

I stopped wagging because his tone was so serious

and because he was looking me full-on in my eyes as if we were doing Focus.

Then I heard a bark I knew as well as my own. Lacey, barking for joy!

I turned to look at the flashing lights and the running children. I could no longer find Lacey's scent, but I knew her direction from her bark. I crouched, ready to run to the end of the leash and jerk it right out of my boy's hand if I had to.

"Sit, Cooper," he said calmly. "You can do this."

8

I did Sit, but I wasn't happy about it. I received a click-and-a-treat for doing Sit, but then we just remained there, not moving. In front of me, so many things were happening, it seemed impossible that I wasn't off leash, scooping up food from the ground and greeting all the people.

I couldn't help but break from Sit yet again, and this time, I did strain at the end of my leash, but my boy said, "No. Come. Sit," and I reluctantly returned to his side.

And so we remained there, not moving, Burke's hand resting lightly on my back.

Was this my life, to do Sit and Stay with my boy, when so many people, and dogs, and Lacey, were running around, and there was all this dropped food to take care of?

Suddenly, I went very still as a thought struck me.

Maybe this *was* my life. I remembered all the times Burke had me remain close to him when there were wonderful activities calling for attention. Right now, I was supposed to be with my boy, not eating hot dogs. I wasn't supposed to be having fun like Lacey, whose scent occasionally danced on the air over to my nose as she mingled and played and ate in the fun crowds.

Maybe I was a different sort of dog.

I couldn't understand all the implications, but it seemed clear to me that Burke wanted something different from me than Wenling wanted from Lacey. My love—yes, of course—but also for me to be a dog who didn't just do Fun.

Sometimes, it seemed, I needed to do *Work*.

I stared up at Burke. I remembered when I first met him, a whole lifetime ago, and how I couldn't understand why he didn't realize I was a dog who lived with other dogs, especially Lacey. Then when I made room in my mind for Burke, deciding he was my boy, I still wanted to be with Lacey, so he somehow had Wenling bring my dog to the Farm—but that didn't mean I went back to living with Mother Dog and the rest of the dog family. Wherever they were, it wasn't on the Farm. Compared to them, *I had a completely different life.*

Now here we were at a place positively designed for dogs, and I so, so wanted to be just like Lacey . . . except I wasn't. I was with Burke. Doing Work.

"Good dog. You're doing Focus, without even being asked," Burke told me. He gave me a click-and-a-treat.

Eventually, Wenling brought Lacey back to our side. She held a piece of hot dog in her hand that she gave to me, and she told me what a good dog I was.

I loved Wenling.

Grant sauntered back to us, reaching down to pet Lacey. I didn't move to receive the same affection, because Burke had told me to do Sit. Because I was *doing Work.* "Hey, Wenling, want to go on the Ferris wheel?" he asked her.

Wenling glanced uneasily at Burke. "But Burke can't . . ."

Burke waved his hand. "Yeah, the chair won't fit on that thing. You guys go on. I'll wait here with the dogs."

Lacey watched in distress as Wenling and Grant strolled over to the giant machine with the buckets. Burke held her leash, which went taut as she strained to follow her girl. But I didn't need restraint—I understood what we were doing now.

I wished I had some way to inform Lacey what I had figured out. I would be happiest if she joined me in doing a silent, patient Sit, but she was whining, glancing at me occasionally as if wondering why I wasn't as upset.

"Someday you'll help me, and I'll get to ride the Ferris wheel," Burke murmured softly. "You and me together, Cooper. They have to let a service dog go wherever I go—it's the law."

I could sense that Burke was a little unhappy. I licked his hand. He rubbed my chest.

"Good boy, Cooper," he said softly.

I nosed Burke's hand to let him know I was there for him. I would *always* be there. I understood now what kind of dog I was.

I was a *working* dog.

A few days later, Burke and Grandma took me for a car ride to a new place, a dog park. Grandma stayed in the car, but Burke and I climbed out. As soon as we did, I smelled dogs. So many dogs! It was hard to stop sniffing the ground and go with my boy to a gate made of wire, but of course I did it, because he asked me to.

On the other side of the gate were Wenling and Lacey!

"Okay!" Burke laughed. That magical, wonderful word meant we were no longer doing Work.

I jumped and whined and pawed at the gate until Burke opened it and let me in. He even let me off my leash so I could run up to Lacey! Lacey and I sniffed each other all over and wrestled chest to chest with our front paws off the ground. I gently nibbled at Lacey's cheek with my teeth, and she broke away to dash around a tree, and I ran after her.

Then a strange feeling came over me. It felt as though chasing Lacey was the wrong thing to do.

How could that be? How could it be wrong to chase my Lacey?

All of a sudden, I realized—it was because I was running away from my boy! We were not at the Farm, where Lacey and I dashed all over together. We were away from home, just like we'd been at the loud, crowded place with the hot dogs. Off the Farm, it felt even more important to be near my boy.

I spun around and dashed back to Burke's chair. Behind me, Lacey barked in confusion, pursuing me and crashing into my side. Lacey was faster than I was, but she didn't know where we were going, so she didn't try to pass me.

"Good boy!" Burke exclaimed when I reached him. *Click*. He tossed me a treat. I snapped it up and looked at him inquiringly. Then I looked at Lacey. Then I looked back at Burke.

"Wow," Wenling admired. "Cooper came back to you on his own. I can't even get Lacey to come when I *call*."

Burke laughed. "I know. It's as if something changed for him in the past twenty-four hours. But the biggest test is coming in just a few minutes."

Wenling frowned. "I have to be honest, I'm a little worried."

Burke nodded. "I get it, but I promise you there won't be a fight. The dog that's coming is all bluster. I just need Cooper to make a choice between me and Lacey."

I was doing a diligent Sit, but Lacey had dashed off and was sniffing at something on the ground. I was a little irritated with her. *We were doing Work.*

"He's sort of made a decision already," Wenling noted.

"Let's just see what happens when Colonel gets here." He nodded at me. "Okay, Cooper. Go have fun."

Lacey and I raced and bounded and tore in circles across the grass. Sometimes other dogs came near us, and we let them play, too, but they were not really important to us.

I was having so much fun, but every so often, as if I felt a tug on a leash, I turned and darted back to check on my boy. When I reached him, I would always hear a click and be handed a delicious treat.

I loved this dog park. I loved Burke and Lacey and Wenling, too. I loved playing, and I loved the clicker.

Then I heard a low, deep growl. Some dogs play-growl when they are excited, but this was not in play.

I spun around. Lacey was backing away from a big dog with rough, shaggy fur. Her ears were up, and her neck was stiff. She was nervous.

The big dog took a stiff-legged step toward her with another, louder growl.

Lacey needed me! I lowered my head and dashed toward her. No one should growl at Lacey. No one should make her afraid.

From behind me, I heard Burke's voice. "Cooper, Come!"

I stopped instantly, torn. Lacey needed me! I *had* to go to her. Lacey was my friend, my dog, my pack. I felt how deep it was in my nature to defend my pack.

But Burke was my boy. And Burke had just told me to do Come in that voice he used when we were doing Work.

I felt a pull toward Lacey and a pull toward Burke, and each pull was as strong as the other.

Which one needed me more? Lacey, of course. She was being challenged by a big, gruff dog. Now, I understood she could take care of herself—I knew from our constant wrestling that Lacey, while not as large as I, was built of solid muscle. But my presence would change everything—there wouldn't even be a fight with two dogs against one.

But which one should I run to? Lacey or Burke? I hesitated, and then I knew the answer.

My boy had called me, and my job to obey him was more important than anything I might want to do as a dog. I spun in my tracks and raced back to my boy. Lacey's frantic barking became more and more distressed behind me.

"Colonel! Here!" another voice called out.

Burke took hold of my collar and snapped a leash on it and with a click fed me a treat and told me I was a good dog. I didn't wag—I felt sad. I had abandoned my Lacey.

Wenling had already run to Lacey and put a leash on her, pulling her away from the big, growling dog. And the big dog, I saw, had stopped menacing Lacey. He had gone to sit by the side of a tall man with a hat, the one who had called out. Burke wheeled over to the man while the dog eyed me coldly. I stared back but didn't growl, because I was doing Work for Burke. Wenling trotted over as well.

"Thanks, Mr. Harris," Burke said to the tall man. "And thanks for bringing Colonel."

"And thanks for calling him away!" Wenling added, petting Lacey to calm her down. Lacey still had a stiff ridge of fur along her back. "I was afraid they were going to fight."

The tall man shook his head. "Colonel doesn't like other dogs, never has. But he won't fight unless the other dog gets into it first. And at the first sign of that happening, I call him and he knows to come, no matter what."

"That's what Cooper's learning," Burke agreed. "That

he's got to come when I call, even if there's dog stuff going on. Even dog stuff with Lacey!"

"They're in love, these two," Wenling explained. "Cooper and Lacey. That's why it's so impressive that Cooper went to Burke instead of helping my dog confront yours."

Lacey was not anxious now, I was glad to see. The rough-looking male dog was still gazing at us with hostility, but both Lacey and I knew he wouldn't try anything with people and two dogs right there.

The man nodded. "Looks like you're doing an excellent job with his training. Good luck with it! I'll take Colonel on home."

The tall man led the angry dog away through the gate, and Burke said, "Okay," and Lacey and I played without leashes holding us back. I still returned to check on Burke occasionally, though. It was as much an instinct for me as lifting my leg on a place where the rough-looking dog had marked.

A few days later, Burke and I were in the driveway. Grant was outside, too, but he was not with us. He was over by the barn, playing with a big ball that he kept throwing up into the air so it went through a metal ring that was stuck high up on one of the barn's walls. He did that a lot, except in the snow.

Burke sat still for a moment, watching his brother. I sat beside him. I had the feeling we were going to do Training, but it seemed we were not starting quite yet.

At last, Burke sighed and turned to put me on a leash that snapped onto the back of my harness. There is something that I always like about being on a leash. I like the feel of it tightening on my chest when I lean into it.

"Okay, Cooper. Time for you to learn how to help me when we're *outside* at school, so I can be with everybody else."

I heard my name and waited patiently. For a time, all we did was sit there watching Grant throw his big ball into the air. Then something wonderful happened: a treat sailed over my head and landed in the grass in front of me!

I didn't know if Burke had tossed it or if it had fallen from the sky, but a treat is a treat no matter what the source. I surged forward but was brought up short by the leash.

"Pull," Burke said quietly.

9

I stared at the treat, so close, right there. Why didn't Burke wheel forward so I could snatch it up? Frustrated, I backed away, then moved forward again to see if the leash had grown any longer. It hadn't, but when I strained, I felt Burke's chair rolling behind me. Encouraged, I kept digging my nails into the ground and eventually made it to the treat.

Click. I gobbled up the small snack and then turned to see why Burke had clicked.

"Good dog," he told me.

I will always accept a click for "good dog." I watched alertly, licking my lips, as Burke raised his hand. Catching a tossed morsel is one of the tricks I do particularly well, and I knew that was what was coming.

But Burke's throw went over my head and bounced in the grass. I was once again held back by the leash.

"Pull," Burke repeated.

The treat was right there! I pressed forward, feeling the harness tighten on my chest. Just as I reached the treat, I heard a click.

Obviously, I was doing something right.

Burke's aim did not improve despite considerable practice. He just couldn't seem to toss the treat within range of my mouth—the snacks always landed in front of me.

Every time I leaned into my harness, Burke's chair rolling behind me, Burke would say, "Pull," and when I reached the treat, I would hear a click.

I was starting to think that *Pull* meant I should walk forward, dragging Burke's chair behind me. It was an odd concept, but there was no denying the click and the treat.

When Burke commanded me to do Pull even without a treat in the grass, it seemed the most natural thing to strain at the harness and feel Burke's chair moving behind me. This also earned me a click-and-a-treat. We did it again, with the same results. And again!

We were doing a Work!

After we'd practiced this for a while, Grant wandered over. He held his ball resting against his hip, and he was sweaty all over, with a smell of salt.

"Hey," he said. "What are you teaching Cooper now?"

I sniffed at Grant's legs. I liked his sweaty smell.

"Focus, Cooper!" Burke said. I turned my head quickly to him and looked in his eyes until he told me, "Okay!" and tossed me a treat.

"I'm teaching him to pull," he told Grant. My ears perked up at the word, but this didn't seem to be a command. Sometimes that happens. "So if my wheelchair gets stuck or something, Cooper can get me out."

"Stuck? At school?"

"Not like in the hallway. Outside, though," Burke explained.

"Outside? Oh, man, I hate to be the one to break it to you, but there's no recess in middle school." Grant snorted.

"I *know* that. But what about maybe we go on a field trip. Or gym class. I won't be able to do those things without Cooper," Burke pointed out.

"You probably won't be able to, anyway. You'll always be in Ms. Hawkins's office or on detention," Grant speculated.

"Oh no, I'm the *good* Trevino brother. Who's Ms. Hawkins?"

"She's the principal, and she's tough. Fair but tough. She's already asked if there's any way I can prevent you from going to her school," Grant said.

"Okay. Sure," Burke replied, rolling his eyes.

"So how's Cooper doing?"

"I think he likes it. He's part malamute, and they're sled dogs. They're bred to pull things."

"That's cool. What's next?"

Burke shook his head. "Nothing more today. We've done about an hour. That's about how long you should work with a dog doing this kind of training. They'll get tired and frustrated if you try to do too much."

Grant nodded. "Just like you. Well, I got to take a shower. Here, catch!" He tossed the ball at Burke. "Shoot some hoops." Grant turned and jogged toward the house.

I looked over at Burke to see if we were playing Fetch now. The ball in his hands was so big, I didn't know how I'd get my mouth around it to bring it back to him, but I would do whatever he wanted me to do.

"Shoot some hoops," my boy muttered.

Suddenly, Burke raised the ball up with both hands and threw it as hard as he could toward the barn. It bounded off a wall and bounced to the ground and rolled away into a bush.

I tensed. Should I chase the ball? Was that what a good dog should do? But Burke did not drop my leash, and when I looked at him, he wasn't paying any attention to the ball anymore. That made me think I was not supposed to chase it this time.

He seemed really, really sad all of a sudden. Angry,

even. I felt like a bad dog. He lowered his hand, and I rubbed the top of my head against it. "You're the only one who really understands how much I want to go to school, how tired I am of being home alone with Grandma all day."

Burke started pushing on the wheels of his chair, propelling himself toward the house. His face was set in a grim look. I paced alongside him, wondering if there was anything I should do to help.

I was still on my leash when we reached the ramp that led up to the porch. I went ahead of Burke, and I felt the harness go tight around my shoulders and chest as I started up.

It was a familiar feeling. It felt like the beginning of Pull.

I glanced back at Burke to see if he would say the word. He still had that unhappy look on his face, but when he saw me, he brightened. "Pull, Cooper!" he commanded.

I threw my weight into the harness and started up the ramp. Pull had suddenly become much harder than it had been down on the driveway! I didn't understand why, but I didn't stop. I just kept going until Burke and I were both on the porch. I was panting. Burke was grinning.

"Good dog, Cooper!" he said, giving me one click and two treats.

I knew I was a good dog. I had done Pull very well, and that's why my boy was happy again.

We did the game with "Pull!" a lot over the next few days, sometimes out in the driveway, sometimes in the house, and sometimes on the ramp. One time when I was doing a very good Pull, Burke suddenly said something new. "Halt!"

I was doing Pull just the same as ever, but suddenly, the chair was not moving. I did Pull harder, digging my claws in, straining my muscles. It wasn't working.

"Halt!" he said again.

Click! I looked back at Burke and got a treat in my mouth. The treat was nice, but I was confused. Were we doing Pull or not?

"I set the brake on the chair," Burke told me. I studied his face, waiting for the word I could understand, the one that would tell me what he wanted. "You've got to learn to stop pulling when I say. Okay, let's go again. Pull!"

I had been *trying* to do Pull! I threw myself forward, and this time, the chair moved easily. What a relief! But a few moments later, the same strange thing happened. "Halt!" Burke commanded, and Pull didn't work anymore.

Click. Treat. What was happening?

We did Pull in this strange new way for a while, and at last, I decided that once Burke said, "Halt!" there was no point in trying to do Pull anymore. It just didn't work. Besides, much as I liked doing Pull, I liked a treat even better, and "Halt!" came with one of those.

When I had gotten very good at both Pull and Halt, Burke and I tried it on a dirt road that ran away from the driveway, through some woods. That was hard! The chair bumped and jolted in and out of ruts, and I had to lean into my harness and dig my claws into the ground to keep us moving forward.

"Such a good dog. I've never been down this road before. Cooper? You're going to take me to a lot of new places! Want to explore?" He undid my leash, and I tensed. "Okay!"

I loved Okay, and I ran all over with my nose to the ground until he called, "Come!" Then I did Pull all the way to the house and back up the ramp, him not telling me to do Halt once.

We entered the living room and saw Grant there, sprawled on a couch. The big ball he'd been playing with the other day was lying next to him.

"Found my ball," he said. "It was under some bushes by the barn."

"Huh," said Burke. "Wonder how it got there."

"Probably got thrown there by some kind of vermin," Grant suggested. "A weasel, maybe. Or a snake."

"Are these the friends you pretend you're playing basketball with, a weasel and a snake?" Burke asked.

Grant grinned at us.

"So," Burke said after a while. "What's middle school going to be like?"

"Huh?" Grant looked puzzled. "Well. It's like, I dunno, school. Classes and kids and lockers and stuff. You know."

"Not really," said Burke. "I don't really know. I've only been homeschooled, remember?"

"Oh. Right." Grant seemed to think a little. "Well, you move around from class to class. Different rooms, I mean. When the bell rings. You know that part. When you get your schedule, I can look at what teachers you get and tell you which are the best ones."

Burke nodded.

"Lunch is the best, because you hang out with your friends. But we don't get that much time for it. So most of the kids come a little early in the morning, and if the weather's okay, we sit on the big stone steps in front. There's room for everybody in the school."

I felt my boy stiffen a little. I looked up at him to see if he needed anything.

"Steps?" Burke asked. "What do you mean?"

"Yeah, the stairs in the front of the school, they're really long and high. So there's kind of like an order to it. The older kids, the eighth graders, sit on the top, and the seventh and sixth graders are closer to the bottom. Everybody just kind of knows where to sit. And . . ." Grant's voice trailed off. "What's up?"

"Steps," Burke said flatly. "How am I supposed to get up the steps?"

Grant frowned. "Well, there's a ramp around the back of the school. The custodian uses it to take out the trash. I know, because Aidan had to use it for a while when he broke his leg, remember?"

"I'm not trash!" Burke snapped.

"Did I say you were trash? Don't be so touchy. What's the big deal?"

"The big deal is you just said that to fit in, I should go sit on the front steps in the morning. And then you said I should sneak up the back ramp when the janitor is emptying the garbage or something. Now you get it?"

"So you don't sit there on the stone steps freezing your fanny off. Big deal." Grant shrugged.

Burke's eyes narrowed. "You do get that this is the first time in my life I'm going to be in a school. That I don't know more than a couple of the kids. That it's going to be really, really hard, and maybe I'm a little nervous already, and now you tell me that instead of hanging out with every other student in school, I'll have to use the trash ramp!"

There was a long silence. Grant shrugged again. "I'll go up the ramp with you. I'll get some of my friends to go with me. How's that?"

Burke looked away from Grant. A long, sad breath came out of his nose. I anxiously looked back and forth between both boys. I got up and began to pace across the rug. I could feel the tension in the room, and it made me restless. Moving helped a little, but not much.

I passed the coffee table with the clicker lying on it. Gently, I picked the thing up in my mouth and brought it over to Burke. I laid it on his lap to remind him that if he was feeling bad, I was always willing to do Work.

I was right—the clicker did make Burke feel better! He looked down at it and laughed just a little. "Okay, silly dog," he said, and reached out to rub my chest. "We can get back to training soon. But there isn't any way you can help me get a wheelchair up stone stairs, is there?"

I wagged. I'd helped my boy. I'd done what I was supposed to do.

Then Burke stopped rubbing my fur. He rolled his chair over to the steps that led up to New Dad's room. He sat very still, and he seemed to be staring at the stairs.

"What do you think, Cooper?" he murmured in a voice only I could hear.

10

Soon after that, we started doing a new Work. It was confusing.

Burke put my harness on me as if we were going for a walk. But we didn't. Instead, he used his arms to boost himself out of his chair and carefully lowered himself to the living room floor. I watched with interest. Except when he was in bed or in the car, I had rarely seen my boy out of his chair.

I nosed him. "Good boy, Cooper," he muttered. He had the clicker in his hand, so I knew we were about to do Training. I was ready. Burke grabbed at my harness with the hand that was not holding the clicker. "Assist!" he told me.

I licked his ear affectionately.

Burke shook his head. He seemed to be waiting for

104

something. *Not this again.* Why did we keep coming up with new Work, and why did it always start with him wanting something from me I didn't understand?

He was staring at the door on the other end of the room, so I turned my head to check out what he was looking at. Was that a crumb of food on the carpet? I took a step in that direction to find out, and Burke hung on to my harness and shoved himself along with his other hand so that he came with me.

Click! I turned my head to look at Burke in expectation, and sure enough, he was digging in his pocket for a treat. He tossed it to me, and I snapped it out of the air.

We did that for a while. *Assist* turned out to mean that I tugged my boy across the floor while he pushed his hand to stay with me. After some days went by, Burke added a new command, "Steady!" That one meant that I held completely still and he leaned on my shoulders while he climbed into and out of his chair.

I was very good at "Assist!" and "Steady!" I knew, because Burke fed me treats and also because I felt the pleasure coming from him when I performed both these tricks. He was happy. I was doing my job. My Work.

I also learned "Pull Right!" and "Pull Left!" These were like doing Pull, except I would steer in one direction or the other. I had trouble keeping the commands straight at first, because they sounded so alike, but eventually I understood. I would do Pull and then Pull

Right and then Halt and we would sit and watch Grant throw the ball that was too big for a dog's mouth at the metal hoop.

One time, Grant turned to Burke. "Want to take a shot?" he asked, holding out the big ball.

"Pass," Burke said dismissively.

"Come on."

Burke's grip on his chair tightened audibly. "You're kidding, right?"

Grant frowned. "No, I was just . . ."

"Sometimes you're a jerk, Grant," Burke snapped. "Pull Left, Cooper."

I hesitated. Which one was Pull Left again? I turned and strained on my harness.

"Left! Pull Left!" Burke shouted.

I could tell from his voice I had gone in the wrong direction. I turned the other way and proceeded until he said, "Pull," which meant go straight.

I loved when I was able to drag the chair behind me, but I was sad whenever Burke was mad at me.

I heard Grant's feet pounding the ground as he ran after us, but I didn't turn. I was doing Work. "Hey, wait up," he panted.

"Halt!" Burke told me.

"Sorry. Okay. I shouldn't have just said to shoot the basket. I don't think I could make a shot sitting in a chair. Okay? I'm apologizing here."

Burke gave Grant a long gaze. "Okay. Sure."

Grant took in a deep breath and let it out. "And I was thinking. Tennis."

"Sorry?"

"Tennis is something you could do. There are wheelchair tennis teams; I looked it up. And the beauty is that you and I could practice together, no one else around. Okay?"

"I don't think so," Burke replied slowly.

"Why *not*? You're constantly saying how much you want to play a sport. Tennis is a sport. Let's just *try it*, Burke."

"Okay," my boy said. "We'll try it."

Okay was only a magic word when he said it to me.

The days grew warmer, and I loved to lie outside in the sun when Burke and I were not doing Training. The warmth soaked into my fur, and sometimes I groaned with delight. Lacey and Wenling came over often. After Lacey and I ran and wrestled, we would lie on the grass, being warm and happy together. At all other times, I felt I was either doing Work or prepared to hear a command to do Work, but when Lacey was with me, I was a dog who played.

As long as Burke told me, "Okay," first.

"How goes the training? Are you going to be ready for school? Coming up pretty soon," Wenling observed.

"A few more things and Cooper will be a full service dog," Burke replied.

Lacey and I both glanced up when Burke said, "Cooper." I loved that Lacey knew my name. Most dogs did not, but then, most dogs were not like Lacey. She was very special.

And every day, we did Assist and Steady, until I sometimes dreamed that I was doing them in my sleep. Then, one day, Burke wheeled his chair to the foot of the stairs and maneuvered himself to the floor. There was a new determination in him. He put one hand on the first stair and reached over to grab my harness.

"The ones at school might be bigger and made of stone, but a step is a step, right? We can do this, Cooper."

I waited eagerly, sensing something was coming.

"Okay, Cooper. Assist!" he told me.

I stared up at the stairs, confused. "Assist!" had never meant going up there before. But I was supposed to take a step forward when Burke said the word, so I did. Hesitantly, I put a foot on the bottom stair. I looked over at Burke. He didn't tell me I was doing Assist wrong, so I climbed more.

When my front feet were on the second stair and my back feet were on the first one, Burke heaved himself up. He was sitting on the bottom stair now, still gripping my harness.

Click. Treat! Well, I didn't know what I had done

to deserve a click, but I was just a dog, and there were many things I didn't understand.

"Assist!" my boy grunted.

I hesitated. This felt wrong. Burke's weight was dragging me backward, nearly pulling me off the stairs. Still, my boy had told me what to do, so I climbed up another step. Burke shoved himself up with me.

Click. Treat!

Again and again, I did Assist up the stairs. We began to develop a rhythm, my boy and me. I climbed; he pushed. We each took a breath and did it again. And again. And each time, the wonderful sound of a click told me I deserved a treat.

"Burke? What's going on?" I heard Grandma say from below us. "Oh, Burke, be careful!"

"Assist!" Burke told me.

One last heave! My boy held on tightly, and I pulled, and we were at the top of the steps. We'd done it!

What we'd done, though, I was less sure of. I could just sense the feeling of triumph coming off my boy.

Grandma was below, staring up speechlessly. Burke grinned down at her. "Now we're ready for school!" he told her, breathing heavily.

"Oh," Grandma said. She wiped at her cheeks and beamed up at us. "Oh, Burke. Oh, Cooper!"

I wagged at her and licked Burke's cheek. Where were we going to go now?

"Burke?" Grandma asked. "Have you and Cooper figured out how to get down?"

"Um," Burke said, looking back down the stairs he
had just climbed. "That's going to be a little tougher. But
the thing is, everyone sits on the steps before school,
not after. So when I leave, I can go out the back, on the
ramp. Cooper only needs to be able to get me up."

"Except you're at the top of the stairs right *now*,"
Grandma pointed out.

Burke nodded. "I didn't think this far ahead."

"I'll go get your father," Grandma said. "Cooper, you
stay right there with Burke!"

A few days later, Grandma drove Grant and Burke
to a wide-open area where heat bounced off
the cement. She parked, and we walked up a long ramp,
and then we were in a fenced-in yard. The fence was
very high around the sides of the yard, which had no
grass, only cement. A sagging fence in the middle was
low enough for me to jump over if I wanted.

"The school doesn't have the money to fix it up, I
guess," Grant noted, "so there's never anybody here.
We've got the whole thing to ourselves."

Burke had me do Sit and Stay in a place where a tall
tree spread a cool shade.

"I'll be back in a little more than an hour," Grandma

called with a wave. I watched her drive away. It made perfect sense to me that I would remain behind with my boy.

Grant pulled out a brightly colored ball and bounced it a few times. I stared at it. He held a club with a wide, flat end and a narrow, hand-size end. Burke held one, too.

"I feel like an idiot," Burke said.

"You're always so good at feeling like yourself," Grant replied. "Okay, you ready?"

"Sure," Burke grunted.

Grant moved the club back and struck the ball, and it sailed over the low fence right at Burke, who raised his own club. "Yaaa!" Burke said. The ball hit his club and veered off. I watched it roll away.

Grant was laughing. "The good news is you can't do any worse than *that*."

"Say, that *is* good news."

"Try again." Grant bounced another ball, and it went over the fence, and Burke waved his club at the air without hitting it.

"One more," Grant called.

This one Burke hit and it rolled right past my nose! I didn't move, though. I was a good dog who knew how to do Stay.

"Okay, Cooper! Bring the balls!" Burke called.

I heard, "Okay," and joyously broke from Stay and

chased down the nearest ball, which was still rolling a little. I loved balls! "Hey, Come!" Burke told me, so I trotted over to him, still chewing the ball. When he held out his hand, I let him take it from me. "Okay!" he said again.

He wasn't throwing the ball he held in his lap, so after a moment, I turned and ran after the first ball. I picked it up and trotted in happy circles.

"You teach him that?" Grant asked.

"Not really," Burke replied. "But he's getting better and better at figuring out exactly what I want."

"Smart dog."

Soon, I had rounded up all the balls, and Burke had them in his lap. I watched eagerly as he picked one up, holding the club in the other.

"Just hit it over. Don't try to ace it," Grant suggested.

Burke swung his club, and the ball dropped to the cement. I scooped it up and took it back to him.

"I'm sort of a natural at this," Burke told his brother.

"Just hit it over."

The next ball made solid contact with the club and soared up and over the big fence. Grant watched it go, pulling his cap off and scratching his head. "Huh," he said.

"Okay, go get it, Cooper!" Burke urged.

I heard the encouragement and ran out the gate and

down the sidewalk and triumphantly grabbed the ball and brought it back.

We played with the balls the whole time, until Grandma returned. "They're all yucky," Grant complained. "Cooper's spit is all over them."

We slid into Grandma's car. "How did it go?" she wanted to know.

"I don't think I'll be trying out for the tennis team," Burke replied.

"Hey, nobody does anything well the first time," Grant argued.

"Oh, I do understand that. But nobody does anything as *badly* the first time, either," Burke noted.

"That's true. It's like you've got no eye-hand coordination at all," Grant admitted. "Like you're the worst in human history."

"Thanks for that, Grant."

Both boys smelled sweaty. What a wonderful day we were having.

"Um, so what about softball?" Grant finally asked.

"What about it?"

"Maybe you'd like that better than tennis, I mean."

Burke nodded. "Great idea. So instead of just missing the ball by myself, I'd be letting down the entire team."

"We'll practice. I'll pitch to you every day before try-outs if you want," Grant offered.

Burke looked out the window. I did, too, but didn't see anything I'd want to chase.

"I get that you're trying to help here, Grant," he finally said softly. "But I can just imagine everyone laughing at me. I would hate that."

They were quiet the rest of the way home.

One very hot day, I did Pull to take Burke down to the pond. I made sure to bark and chase all the ducks away. While I was doing that, my boy slid himself of his chair and sat on the dock. I figured we were about to do Assist yet again, or maybe Steady, so I went over to be close to him.

Burke pulled his shirt off over his head and tossed it on the warm boards. Then he told me to do Assist until he was sitting right on the edge of the dock. Carefully, he maneuvered his legs so they were hanging down toward the water.

Then he braced his hands on the boards and fell down into the pond. The water closed over his head.

My boy was gone!

11

Burke needed me, and I did not hesitate. I flung myself off the dock and into the water with a huge splash.

Instantly, my fur was cold and heavy. I ignored the drag and swam with all my strength to where the ebbing ripples told me my boy had slipped into the murky water.

I searched desperately. I could not see my boy anywhere, and I could not smell him, either. What should I do? Where was Burke? A whimper broke from my lips.

There! His head popped out of the water not too far from me. I paddled vigorously toward him, but he reached out to grab my collar, steering me away from climbing up on top of him to save him. "No, Cooper, stay back," he panted. "Good dog. I'm okay. Don't push me under. Ow, don't scratch me!"

I whined a little and pressed forward, but he kept me at arm's length. We drifted in the pond, and I began to feel better. Burke's voice was calm. His hand was steady. He was all right. That helped me relax.

"See, boy, it's fine. We're swimming!" Burke laughed and let me go. He stretched out to float on his back and reached out his arms. I paddled in a circle around him, needing to be close, but I now understood that my boy was not in trouble.

"Doesn't matter that I can't walk, when I'm in the water, Cooper," he whispered to me. "Here I'm just like everybody else."

He rolled over and paddled with his arms. We were both swimming, and I realized that my boy was happy in the water. He felt free.

And I was with him. So we could feel free together. And those ducks didn't dare come to the pond while I was there.

After our swim, my boy pulled himself up to the ladder on the dock and hoisted himself up. I paddled to shore and climbed out of the water to the dock and did Assist to help him back to his chair, and then Pull up to the house.

"Grant!" Burke called as soon as we were through the front door.

Grant strolled out of the kitchen, a cookie in his hand. I stared at it as he raised it to his lips. "Your hair is wet," he noted.

"Thank you."

"Your *dog* is wet."

"This is all very helpful, and I'll dry him in a minute, but would you listen to me? I know something I can already do, something I didn't have to learn from scratch. Not like tennis or hitting a softball," Burke said urgently. "Something I've been doing since *birth*."

"Pooping?" Grant guessed.

"*No.* Not that."

"You've been pooping since birth," Grant reasoned. "It was the first thing I noticed about you."

"I'm talking about a *sport*," Burke said impatiently.

"You were actually pretty good at pooping. You could get into the Olympics."

"Grant. Stop. *Swimming.* Swimming is what I've been doing!" Burke announced happily. "And you know I'm fast—I can beat you in the water, and I can't even kick with my legs."

"Probably I let you win," Grant decided. "Otherwise, I'm afraid you'll poop in the water like a baby."

"How can I be so much more grown-up than you are when I'm younger?" Burke demanded.

I slept very well that night, tired out by all that Work.

*   *   *

In the morning, things were very predictable . . . until they weren't.

It was one of those mornings where Grant ran around looking for things, and New Dad ate breakfast quickly. Grant said, "School," and New Dad said, "Work," and Grandma said things like, "Anybody would think you'd never gotten ready for school before in your life, Grant! Where's your backpack? Where are your gym shoes?"

So soon, they would leave and Burke would sit with Grandma, and I would lie at their feet and wish we could do anything else.

Or so I thought.

Unlike other mornings, Burke seemed to be just as busy as Grant. I followed him closely as he wheeled from room to room, picking things up and putting them in a soft sack that sat on his lap.

My boy was nervous. I could feel it in him, a tension in his muscles and his voice and deep down inside him, too. Something was happening. So I stayed nearby to be sure I'd be a part of whatever it was.

When Grant left, we all went with him for a car ride in the truck!

It was a warm morning. Grandma smelled like the

bacon she had fed the boys but not me for breakfast. I barked at a dog out of the window. Then we passed a goat farm, and I barked at that, too.

"Don't be nervous," Grant told Burke. "Just tell the teachers you're my brother. They all love me."

"I tell them you're my brother, they'll send me straight to the principal's office," Burke replied.

I saw a squirrel!

"Cooper! Stop barking, you idiot!" Burke laughed. I wondered if he was trying to tell me he had also seen the squirrel.

Grandma stopped the car, and Grant jumped out. I watched with interest as he walked around the back to get Burke's chair and did a human version of Steady to help Burke slide into it. We were in front of a large building with a set of wide stone stairs in front of it. Boys and girls Burke's age, some maybe a little older, were sitting and standing on the steps, talking and laughing. A few of them were tossing a football back and forth. That looked very interesting to me. I would be glad to be a part of that.

But then Burke called me, and I knew we were doing Work, not chasing a football. I bounded out of the car to his side.

"Okay. Well," Grant said.

Burke was looking at the other kids on the steps, and the tension that had been in him all morning was rising.

"Go on, Grant. Climb up to be with the other seventh graders. I don't need a babysitter."

"Right." Grant shook his head. "Okay, little brother. You're on your own."

Burke reached out and gripped my collar. "No, I'm not. Cooper's with me."

I watched curiously as Grant strode away from us. When he reached the stone stairs, children Burke's age moved out of the way so that he had a path to the middle, where older boys and girls made room for him to sit. Burke let go of my collar, took a deep breath, and started wheeling himself toward the steps.

The chattering ceased. I paced myself to match Burke's slow speed as we approached the gathering of youngsters. Then he stopped wheeling. I glanced up at him and saw him smiling just a little. He took hold of my leash. "Cooper, Pull!"

I instantly understood. I leaned into my harness and did Pull toward the steps. The wheelchair followed behind me, and I noticed that all the children were watching us. The boys with the football stopped throwing it and stared.

We reached the bottom of the stairs, and I had already stopped before Burke said, "Halt!" I knew what was coming.

"Hey," a boy standing there said uncertainly. "Um . . . so you know the ramp is in the back, right?"

"I know," Burke agreed, "but I think I'll go up and sit with friends."

"Okay," the boy said uncomfortably, "but how are you going to, you know, get up the steps?"

Burke grinned. "Watch!" he invited.

I did Steady while Burke slid out of his chair. He gripped my harness and braced himself on the stairs with his other hand. "Assist!" he told me.

Step by step, up we climbed. Kids moved aside to make room. I smelled wonderful meats and cheeses on some of them, but I was focused on Assist. I glanced up and saw that Wenling was sitting a few steps away, smiling down at us. I wagged for her, and soon we reached her side.

"Well, hi, Burke," Wenling greeted casually.

"Hey," Burke said, breathing a little harder than usual. He looked around. "Think someone could get my wheelchair?" he asked nobody in particular.

I greeted Wenling happily while the boy who had talked to Burke at the bottom of the stairs grabbed the chair and brought it up to us. "Cool dog!" he said enthusiastically. "Did you train him to do that?"

"Yeah," Burke answered.

I buried my nose in Wenling's hair and sniffed hard. She smelled like Lacey. I looked around, but I did not spot Lacey anywhere. That was strange. Had Wenling come to this place without Lacey? What was the point of having a dog if you don't take the dog everywhere?

Many children were around us now. Burke said, "Okay, Cooper," so I knew I could relax. Hands reached out to pet me. A girl scratched at the base of my tail, and I moaned with pleasure.

"What's his name?"

"Cooper."

"Good dog, Cooper!"

"Hi, Cooper!"

Burke put an arm around my shoulders and buried his face in my fur. "Thanks, Cooper," he whispered. "You make me the coolest kid in school. I can sit on the steps with a *dog*."

I liked this new place. I liked the friendly children, and I liked Wenling (even without Lacey by her side), and I liked that my boy was happy.

And then something changed.

A woman pushed through the big doors that led into the building. She had on dark shoes with tall heels that went *clack* as she descended the stone steps. She stared at my boy and me.

"What is going on?" she said. "Why is this dog here?"

The way she said *dog* made it sound like the word *bad* was in front of it. The children stopped petting me. Most of them moved away.

Burke looked up. "Cooper's mine. My service dog. I'm Burke. Burke Trevino."

"Service dog?" the woman asked. "No one told me about any service dog."

"Oh," Burke said. "It's okay. Cooper comes with me everywhere. It's his job. I didn't know I was supposed to tell anybody. He's not a problem. He's really well trained."

"Trained to do what?"

"He got Burke up the stairs!" the boy who'd carried the wheelchair exclaimed. "It was really cool!"

The woman looked at him, and he seemed to shrink a little. "Justin Paulsen, is the dog yours?" she asked.

The boy shook his head.

"Then I don't think we need your help with this conversation, do we?"

The boy shook his head again. He gave Burke a sympathetic look before he backed away.

"Cooper helps me up the stairs, and he pulls me when I need it," Burke said to the woman.

"So you are unable to wheel yourself in your chair?" challenged the woman.

Burke looked confused. "Huh? No, not *unable*, but—"

"Cooper helps Burke with a lot of things," Wenling interrupted. "He's really good at his job."

I was happy to hear Wenling's voice. I wagged at her.

"I can understand why the stairs might be difficult.

That's why we have a ramp in the back, for disabled students. Perhaps you were not aware."

Burke was silent for a moment. "I know about the ramp. But in the morning, all the students sit out here and talk. It wouldn't be fair if I couldn't be with them."

The woman pursed her lips. "Well, Burke, as I often tell my students, life isn't always fair."

Burke lifted his eyes challengingly. "Oh, I know all about *that*."

No one was speaking, but there was a rustling noise as they stirred.

"I suppose you do," the woman finally said. "I apologize for implying otherwise." Then she frowned. "But I don't like things being sprung on me out of nowhere. And this has got to be the largest dog I've ever seen in my life. He looks like a wolf."

"He's part malamute, that's why," Burke volunteered. "And I'm sorry I didn't know to call you. It's my first day in a school—I've always been homeschooled before."

"Yes, I was made aware of that. But I wasn't told about the giant dog."

"But Burke can keep Cooper with him at school, can't he, Ms. Hawkins?" Wenling asked anxiously.

12

There was a long wait, with no one saying anything. It sounded as if Burke was holding his breath. Finally, the woman nodded. "For now, I suppose, the dog can stay. He must be on a leash whenever he is on school grounds. A *short* leash. He must never be in a position to lunge at other students. This is for right now, while I look into the matter."

"Oh," Burke started to object, "Cooper would never *lunge—*"

"Meanwhile," the woman interrupted, raising her voice, "the bell's about to ring, so I suggest everyone head in. *And I do not want to hear of anyone attempting to play with this dog.* He is a service animal. Let him do his job."

She turned and clacked up the stairs, and as she did, an enormously loud bell clanged, and I looked around to see where it was coming from. Burke laughed a little and rubbed my neck. "You're so good with loud noises!" he told me.

"You trained him well. Lacey would probably freak out," Wenling observed.

I glanced at her when she said Lacey, but then snapped to attention when Burke gripped my harness and told me to do Assist.

The other boy carried the chair to the top, and I did Steady, and Wenling held the door open so that Burke could wheel himself inside the building, and of course I stayed with him, close to his side.

The hallways were just as full of children as the steps had been. Burke and Wenling and I picked our way around all the moving bodies, and children on all sides reached out to touch my fur as we passed.

"Nice dog!" many of them said. Lots of the hands smelled like other dogs.

"His name's Cooper," Burke said, wheeling himself along.

"Good dog, Cooper!"

We found our way to a room full of tables and children. Wenling waved and continued on to a different room. A man about Grandma's age came over to talk to us and admire what a good dog I was being, doing Sit and Stay next to Burke's chair.

"If you two are here for history, you've come to the right place. I'm Mr. Kindler."

"Hi, Mr. Kindler. This is Cooper, and I'm Burke."

"I hope you'll both work hard in my class. So, does Principal Hawkins know about this?"

"Um. She does now," Burke said.

The man shrugged and smiled. "Fine by me. What kind of dog is he?"

"We think maybe malamute and something else, Great Dane, maybe," Burke said.

"No wonder he's so big." The man rubbed my head and went to stand at the front of the class and talk to the children. Burke sat, and I patiently did Sit next to him.

It was strange to be at a table so long without any food showing up. I could smell some ham in a pack hanging on the back of a boy's chair close by, but when I'm on Stay, I'm not allowed to investigate such things.

After a while, I circled and lay down with a yawn, but I jumped up when that bell rang again, especially when all the children in the room rose from their chairs like the ducks flying away from the pond. Burke and I made our way back out into the hall and then into another room, where we did Sit and Stay some more. *Click*. Treat!

All the Stay seemed a little pointless to me, but Burke was happy. I could tell by the way he was sitting and breathing and smiling down at me, the way his hand stroked my ears every now and then. Whatever I was doing here, if it made him happy, I was willing to do it all day long.

And we did. All day long. Sit and Stay in this room, Sit and Stay in that. There was one room where delicious smells made my mouth water and the children talked and laughed and ate and threw me treats. I wagged as I snatched them out of the air.

"Please don't feed him. He's working," Burke said.

Suddenly, the children didn't seem to like me as much. They still smiled and called my name, but no more treats were tossed my way.

Finally, that bell rang one last time, and all the kids crowded out into the hallway. They seemed more excited this time, and I didn't know why—it was just the hallway. We'd been in it a lot.

Burke steered me toward the door that led to the place with the food smells. He pushed through to the back, where a long ramp like the one at the Farm led down to the grass. I lifted my leg and left my mark on a tree, and then we spotted the car with Grandma in it. I did Steady so Burke could get into the car and then bounded in myself. Grant put the chair in the back.

Everyone talked, and I watched carefully out the window for squirrels as we drove home.

After that, we went to the building with the stone steps almost every day. I came to understand that it was called School. We were doing School.

Lots of children talked to me and petted me. The boy Burke called Justin met us on the steps most mornings to say hello to me and to take Burke's wheelchair up the stairs. He would always tell me, "Good dog," and he started bringing dog treats in his pockets and giving me one after Burke said, "Okay."

I liked doing Okay.

Some of the grown-ups liked to pet me as well. But the woman with the loud, clacking heels on her shoes did not pet me. I noticed that her hands and her skirts smelled like cats. I didn't really like the smell being so strong on a person, when other odors, like peanut butter, are so much more attractive.

Despite my misgivings about the cat smells, I wagged when the clacking woman came up to me one morning, just after all the children had bolted off the steps as the big bell rang. I'll wag for anybody.

"Excuse me, Burke. A moment, please."

"Yes, Ms. Hawkins?"

We stopped in the big hallway, and children flowed around us on either side. Many of them glanced at us, but no one called to me or offered a kind hand or a treat.

I didn't understand why people were ignoring us all of a sudden.

"Where did you tell me your dog received its service animal training?" the woman asked.

Burke went still. "I trained him myself, Ms. Hawkins."

The woman nodded. "That's what I've heard. Well, that makes a big difference, don't you think? Cooper's not *really* a service dog."

I looked at Burke, who seemed suddenly to be upset. Was this lady making him feel that way?

"Everyone says I did a good job," Burke replied quietly.

The loud bell rang again, and now the hallway was empty.

"Look, Burke," the woman said, leaning down and lowering her voice. "I don't think you realize the problems that come with my job. You'll understand when you're older, but middle school can be a particularly challenging time for students and faculty alike. My budget's been cut, and I'm trying to manage things with a short staff. Do you understand what I'm trying to say to you here? I'm barely in control. Your dog makes my task very difficult."

Burke didn't reply.

After a moment, the woman straightened. "Trained him yourself," she said with a firm nod. "I think that *does* make a difference."

I was glad when the woman clacked off down the hallway, her odors trailing her like a pack of cats.

When my boy was excited or nervous, I could smell it on him, jumping right off his skin. When New Dad took Grant and Burke and me on a long, long car ride, I could sense both boys feeling that way—even New Dad seemed anxious, and he didn't get stirred up about *anything*.

"I guess I didn't know Saginaw was so far away," Burke remarked at one point. We were going too fast for me to spot anything worth barking at, and the windows were rolled up.

"It's okay, Burke. Either Grandma or I can drive you to swim practice every Saturday," New Dad reassured him.

"And in a few years, I'll have my license, and then I can drive you," Grant added.

"Great. I've always wanted to be in a car crash," Burke replied.

"This will be fun," New Dad said after a long silence. Burke didn't reply.

We finally stopped so I could lift my leg on one of several parked cars that were lined up outside a big building. When we pushed inside, a strong, eye-watering smell hit me.

"I guess we know which way is the pool," Grant observed.

We went into a room full of metal boxes like those in the hallways at the school. Burke changed clothes and sat on a bench under a nozzle and got wet. I sniffed him curiously.

There was an indoor pond on the other side of an open door to a *huge* room with a high ceiling. "I'm Coach Barger," a hairless man with a whistle around his neck told us. I was paying less attention to him and more to several dogs who were patiently doing Sit. There were many people New Dad's age on wooden steps. Some children were swimming in the water. I wondered if this was some sort of strange dog park.

"Sorry if we're a little late," New Dad apologized.

"Not at all. Not at all," the hairless man replied. "So you're Burke. Ready to show us what you've got?"

"Sit, Cooper. Stay," Burke told me.

This was exactly what I did not want to hear, but I did as instructed. The other dogs were ignoring me, concentrating on the children in the pond, so I ignored them.

Hairless Head blew a blast on his whistle. "Line up for some speed trials!"

The children found their way to the cement side of the pond. Burke slid into the water without Assist, and

Grant pulled his chair back. I had no idea what we were doing and was uneasy that Burke was in the pond.

"On my mark!" Hairless Head shouted.

Everyone went tense, even New Dad. I glanced to see if any of the other dogs understood what was happening. One of them broke Sit, clearly picking up on the mood in the big room, but apparently we were all on Stay.

There was an ear-piercing blast from the whistle, and everyone in the water began splashing, making their way swiftly to the far end of the pond.

"Come on, Burke!" Grant shouted.

Several of the people New Dad's age also yelled, but New Dad spoke very quietly. "Go, Burke, you can do it."

When the children made it to the far end, they realized how much they missed the dogs and turned around and headed back. They passed Burke, who hadn't turned around yet—he was still swimming for the far end. I wagged, thinking he must be having fun.

Though they all started at the same time, the children decided to return and stop at our end of the pond at different intervals. Burke wanted to wait the longest— long after everyone else was panting and holding the cement sides, he was still splashing his way toward us.

Hairless Head turned to New Dad. "Not bad. I need

to help him with his crawl—his head should be down. Does he do any other strokes? Butterfly?"

New Dad looked to Grant, who shook his head.

"Well, no matter," said the man as he raised his whistle to his lips. With a blast, he shouted, "Laps! Let's go!"

Burke held on to the side of the pond, and I couldn't help myself; I broke Stay and went to lower my nose to him. He seemed very sad. "It's okay, Cooper," he said hoarsely.

My boy was very quiet on the car ride back home. His skin smelled powerfully of the strange water from the indoor pond.

"Hey," New Dad said after a long silence. "There's a YMCA in Gaylord. You can practice there, get your speed up."

No one said anything for a while. I spotted a brown animal, larger than a dog, bounding away from the side of the road, but it happened so fast I didn't have a chance to bark. I wondered if I should go ahead and bark anyway, even though I had lost sight of it.

"It's your fault, Grant," Burke blurted suddenly.

Grant drew back in surprise. "My fault?"

"You *let* me win. You *let* me think I was fast. But I'm worse than everyone," Burke accused bitterly.

"Everyone in that pool has been practicing, son," New Dad responded reasonably.

"I don't mind not being the best. But I hate being the absolute *worst*," Burke replied. He was so upset I did Focus, trying to help.

"The coach said he could help you with your stroke," Grant said.

"I'm not going back," Burke replied tersely.

We bounced up the dirt driveway. "Can you watch Cooper? I need to be alone for a minute," Burke said as I did Steady so he could get into the chair.

"Sure," Grant said. "Stay, Cooper."

Grant grabbed my leash, and I watched in bewilderment as my boy wheeled off toward the pond.

13

"That didn't go well," New Dad remarked as he stood next to Grant.

"I don't get it. It's like if he can't win, he gives up," Grant complained.

New Dad nodded thoughtfully. "Well, think how things look from his point of view. He's been hearing his whole life that his older brother is a 'natural athlete,' and it does seem you excel at many things rather effortlessly." New Dad held up a hand. "I know what you're going to say, that it takes a lot of practice, but most of that work you do with your teammates after school, and he doesn't see any of it. To him, it appears you're just immediately good, and he wants that experience for himself."

I saw Burke wheel out onto the dock. Was he going to chase ducks without me?

"I guess I shouldn't have let him beat me at swimming," Grant said.

"Oh, don't blame yourself. You were just trying to help Burke get past this sense that he's bad at everything," New Dad replied. "And anyway, I've got a surprise coming tomorrow that will cheer him up. Something that will change everything."

When Grandma drove us home from school the next day, New Dad was waiting for us in the living room. Grant and Burke and I stopped as soon as we were inside, staring at the thing in the middle of the room.

It was another chair with wheels, but the wheels were smaller than the ones on my boy's chair. New Dad and Grandma were smiling widely, and Burke looked amazed. I sniffed the thing to see if I could find out why everyone was so excited, but that didn't give me any new information.

"Whoa," Burke said. "Is that . . . a motorized wheelchair?"

"It sure is!" New Dad said, grinning. "Want to try it out?"

"Yeah!" Burke answered.

He wheeled himself over to the new chair, and I did Steady so he could switch from the old chair to this new one. I looked around. Were we done now?

"Let's see how fast it can go!" Burke suggested, grinning, and he touched a little lever that stuck up from the arm of the chair.

He shot forward! I backed up in alarm. I'd never seen a wheelchair move without my boy pushing on the wheels or me doing Pull. But this one was moving all by itself!

"It's okay, Cooper!" Burke shouted, and he zoomed out into the hallway. "Man, this thing is fast!"

We all crowded into the hallway to watch him reverse and turn around and come back toward us. "I'll have to watch my toes!" Grandma laughed.

"I want to try it outside," Burke told everyone.

New Dad opened the door, and Burke shot down the ramp to the driveway. I galloped after him. Burke sped back and forth and spun in circles, grinning.

I waited for us to start Training, but that didn't seem to be happening. Burke just zipped around while New Dad and Grandma watched and I sat there by myself.

From that point on, Burke traveled everywhere in his new chair. I went with him, of course, because that's what I did—but there didn't seem to be much Work for me to do.

There was no Pull. We didn't do Assist on any stairs. My boy seemed happy, and I knew that should make me happy, too. But I was his dog! I needed to do Work!

After two days of Burke playing with his new chair

and not with his dog, it was a do School morning again. We all piled into the car, and I noticed with distaste that the new chair was in the back.

When we arrived, Burke didn't ask me to do Pull over to the steps. But I did do Assist up to Wenling, which made me feel better. The new chair, I noticed, was heavier than the old one. Both Justin and Grant had to wrestle it up to the top of the steps, where it sat until that loud bell announced it was time to cram into the hallways.

We went to our first room to do Sit and Stay, just the same as always. Mr. Kindler, the man who lived in that room, said hi to me as he usually did. I had just settled down next to Burke's table when the door opened and the woman in tall, dark heels clacked into the room. I had learned that her name was Ms. Hawkins.

"Burke Trevino," she said, looking blandly at my boy, "I'd like to speak to you in my office, please. Bring the dog."

All the children glanced at one another.

"Settle down," Mr. Kindler advised.

We cruised out the door and down the hallway after Ms. Hawkins. The new chair made an irritating, though nearly silent, humming noise when it moved.

We ended up in a room with a big desk in it. Ms. Hawkins sat on one side of the desk, and Burke sat on the other. I could smell cats very strongly in this room, and I looked around alertly, but I did not spot any. Cats are like squirrels in that regard.

"I see you have a new wheelchair," Ms. Hawkins said to Burke.

Burke nodded. "Yeah, I just got it this weekend."

"It seems easier for you to get around with it," Ms. Hawkins observed.

Burke nodded again.

"So the dog is no longer needed," Ms. Hawkins went on. "This will be the last day you'll bring it to this school."

Burke stared. "*What?*"

"I have been extremely patient, but that dog is disruptive," Ms. Hawkins went on. "He's all anyone talks about. And he's huge. I hate to think what would happen if he bit someone."

"Cooper would never bite anyone! He's been socialized since he was a little puppy," Burke objected hotly. He sounded angry. I looked around for what was bothering him. Maybe he didn't like the smell of cat?

"So you say. I can't take that risk."

Burke folded his arms. "There is no risk."

"That is not for you to determine, young man. It's my decision. I understand some people won't like it, but I am not here to be popular."

There was a long silence. I wanted to get up and pace, but I knew I was supposed to do Stay by Burke's chair. I yawned anxiously.

The woman's face softened just a little. "Look. I understand that you've been homeschooled for the past several years. I'll do everything in my power to make sure you're caught up to the level of the other students. But that requires that you follow the rules. This is a *school*, Burke. The same rules apply to everyone."

"I don't need to get caught up," Burke said. "I take the same tests as everybody else. I always get an A. But I need my dog with me. He's not just a service dog. He's an emotional support dog, too."

Ms. Hawkins snorted a little. "Oh, come now. I'm sure every child here would like to bring their pets in, but it's just not possible. Suppose someone tomorrow wants to bring in their emotional support lizard? Or a gerbil? You see how quickly things would get out of control. We had a child a few years ago who cried every morning saying goodbye to her cat. Her mom begged, but we couldn't let her bring her pet to school. We have to draw a line."

She reached into a drawer of her desk and took something out that made me snap to attention. She put it on the edge of her desk, very close to Burke and me. "I didn't want the situation to get this far, but I've been reading up on service animals, and—"

Cheese! She'd put a little piece of cheese on the edge of the desk, just for me! This cat-smelling, clack-walking woman was nicer than she seemed. I jumped forward and snapped the treat up. Cheese is delicious!

"There you go," Ms. Hawkins said smugly. "A service dog should be able to ignore a treat unless given permission to take it. Your dog can't do that. It's not an actual service dog."

"That's not fair. He hasn't been trained for that."

"Because you trained him at home, yourself. He didn't go to a certified academy. A working dog should ignore food under all circumstances—that's in the guidelines I've read. So he's not really a service animal at all, and your new chair gives you access to everywhere you need to go. I've made my decision. The animal may not spend any more time in my school."

Burke folded his arms. "Then I won't spend any more time here, either. My grandma can go on homeschooling me."

"If you keep homeschooling, you'll just fall further and further behind," Ms. Hawkins warned.

Burke snorted. "I'm already ahead of most of the other kids in reading and math. And that's *because* I'd been homeschooled. Are we done here?"

Ms. Hawkins frowned. "Don't be rude, young man. Being in that chair does not give you liberties to speak to me like that. And yes, we are done."

"Cooper, Come."

Burke pressed the lever, and his new chair scooted him out of the room. I checked to be sure there was no more cheese before I followed. We went back to do Sit and Stay some more, but I could tell Burke was unhappy. I nosed at his hand a lot, and he'd pet me each time I did, but it didn't seem to make him feel any better.

That night, everyone sat around the kitchen table and talked. They said my name a lot, but nobody gave me any treats.

"Well, son, I don't like how Ms. Hawkins handled it, but maybe she does have a point," New Dad observed. "You *can* manage at school without Cooper."

I wagged, but nobody noticed.

"Yeah, I can get around," Burke argued, "but it's not the same, Dad. When Cooper's there, I'm the kid with the cool dog. Without him, I'm just the kid in the wheelchair."

"Burke's right," Grandma agreed. "He's done all this work training Cooper, and he should have some reward from that. Cooper *is* a service dog, and that principal doesn't get to decide otherwise."

New Dad nodded reluctantly. "Well, all right, I'll call the school and see what I can do."

"She's not going to agree to let Cooper in," Burke warned.

"Maybe not, but it's the next step. If she still says no . . . well, then, I don't know what we'll do."

"Take her to court!" Grant exclaimed.

"Right!" Burke agreed.

"I sure hope it doesn't come to that. And anything involving the law takes time, Burke."

"It's worth it," my boy insisted.

Grandma patted Burke's hand. "That's all right. We'll go back to homeschooling while we wait."

After that day, we didn't do School anymore. Wenling and Lacey still came over to visit many afternoons, and that was fun, especially when Burke said, "Okay!" and I could run and wrestle, but I missed Justin and all the other kids at School who petted me and talked to me and told me, "Good dog." I missed doing Assist up the steps and Pull down the hallways.

But there was other Work for me. One day, he told me to do Focus, and then he held a chicken treat under a big leather glove, the kind of glove that Grant and Burke would wear when they threw a ball to each other in the yard. I loved that game because when one of the boys missed, I would chase the ball down and leap on it, and then it was *my* ball.

But there was no ball in the glove now—only the treat. And Burke just sat there, even though we both knew where the treat was. Finally, I decided it was up to me, and I tried to nose the glove away.

"Leave It!" Burke snapped.

I was baffled. What did that mean? I tried to nose the glove aside again, and Burke snapped the same words at me. "Leave It! No! Leave It!"

No? No to a *treat?* What did he think a chicken treat was *for?* "Leave It!" he commanded again, and this time he handed me a *different* treat—a liver-flavored one.

Click.

After we repeated this strange action several more times, I decided to wait Burke out. I sat down and stared at him, ignoring the chicken treat under the glove. And it worked! He made a click and tossed me the liver treat! Liver is not as good as chicken, but with this madness going on, it seemed that liver was the best I was going to get.

After a few days of this, I learned to cheat by pretending I did not care about the treat under the glove or a hat or one of Burke's scarves—it was amazing how many things he could come up with to put over treats. "Leave It!" he would say, and I'd turn my nose away as if I didn't care one bit about the delectable-smelling thing that he'd hidden away. I'd get a click and some liver.

Liver I was allowed to eat was better than chicken I wasn't.

Eventually, I figured out that when Burke said, "Leave It!" the best thing to do was stare right at his hand. That's where the treats were *actually* coming from.

Leave It was usually an inside game, but Get It was different. That one we started playing *outside*.

"Come, Cooper!" Burke said as he hummed out the door and down the ramp. I followed and saw that Burke had scattered a few items over the lawn—a shoe, a ball, a stick, a sock. They all looked excellent for chewing.

"Get It!" Burke told me.

I had no idea what he meant, and who wanted to try to figure it out when there were so many things around to chew? I pounced on the stick and shook it.

"Leave It," Burke told me.

I stared at him in disbelief. Leave It? A *stick*?

"Leave It," he repeated.

So I dropped the stick. He pointed at a ball. "Get It!" he told me.

Whatever. I picked up the stick again. "Leave It!" I dropped it.

I had no idea what we were doing.

14

I decided to lift my leg and mark a flower and hope Burke would Leave It this new game of Get It.

"Get the ball! Get It!"

The day was warm, the grass was soft, and I would have really loved to roll over on my back and take a nap. But it seemed that Burke did not want to celebrate this lovely day with a fun stick. I licked his fingers to let him know that I still loved him despite his crazy behavior.

Maybe if I carried the ball over to him, he'd throw it for me and forget this weird Get It stuff.

So I did that, and Burke was very happy. There was even a click and a *chicken* treat in it for me. He threw the ball and yelled, "Get It!" and I pounced on it (of course I did! It was a ball!) and that's how that went, until he threw the hat, and then finally the stick.

I finally figured out that Get It wasn't just about balls—it was about whatever my boy needed.

And about treats for me, of course.

I was so happy to have learned new Work and so unhappy when we stopped doing it. Burke had his new humming chair, and chasing him in it wasn't nearly as fun as doing Pull Left or Pull Right or even Halt. I was a dog who did Work; that was my purpose. Except Burke didn't have much Work for me anymore. I longed to go back to the stone steps, to do Assist.

Sometimes Burke or Grandma still said, "School," and my ears would perk up, but we never went to do School. They just sat at the kitchen table and looked at books or tapped on plastic boxes, and sometimes Burke groaned.

I lay on the ground beside my boy in his new chair and sighed long sighs, but he didn't seem to notice I was there. He didn't need anything from me.

One day, I became so bored that I went into Burke's bedroom and picked up one of his shoes, which was lying by the bed. It smelled like my boy, and that was comforting. I started to chew.

After a while, Burke and his humming chair came

whizzing in, and Burke took the shoe away from me. He spoke in a loud voice, and I could tell he was unhappy with me for some reason.

I looked away from his face and waited for his anger to be over. Maybe then we'd do some Training or something interesting. But we didn't. Burke zoomed out of the room, and I heard him talking to Grandma. "Look what Cooper did to my shoe!"

"That's not like Cooper," Grandma said. She came in to look at me. "Cooper, do you need to go out? What's wrong?"

She didn't say any of the words I wanted to hear— Pull or Steady or Assist. I'd even be glad to hear Leave It or Stay.

She shook her head and went back to the kitchen. I wandered in and sat down and stared hard at my boy, doing a perfect Focus, but he was tapping on that plastic thing and didn't even glance at me.

I wandered restlessly around the kitchen. I nosed at a door of a cabinet to see if it would open. It didn't. I returned to the kitchen and lifted my leg and directed a stream of pee right at a table leg.

"Cooper!" Burke yelled. My ears perked up. He'd noticed me! "Cooper, bad dog!"

I knew it was a bad dog thing to pee in the house, and I felt ashamed, but at the same time, I was glad to have my boy's attention. He was focused on me, and for once, he'd left those papers and books alone.

"Cooper, outside!" Grandma said, and she took me by the collar and hustled me out of the kitchen door. "Burke, get some paper towels. What was that about?"

The door slammed behind me as I stood in the grass with my head hanging down. I waited and waited, but Burke did not come out to do Training with me, and we didn't go to School.

Too many days like this passed. Then came a day where all the people started saying some new words over and over. "Happy birthday!" Grandma said to Burke as he wheeled into the kitchen in the morning.

"Happy birthday!" New Dad said, too. I began to wonder if this was a new kind of command, and they were expecting Burke to do something when they said it. But all he did was smile, and no one gave him a treat, not even liver.

In the afternoon, Burke and Grant and Grandma and New Dad were all in the living room and Burke was pulling paper off some boxes when the doorbell rang. I could smell Wenling and Lacey, and so I barked to let everyone know that it was time to be excited, and I ran to the door with my tail wagging.

Grandma opened the door, and Wenling and Lacey were on the other side. And so was Ava! Lacey and I flung ourselves down the steps to race through the grass, and I heard Wenling say that same "Happy birthday!" thing, for whatever reason.

"Hi, Wenling. Hello . . . Ava," Burke greeted awkwardly.

"You have to come out to the barn!" Wenling said. "Grant and I have a present for you there."

Lacey jumped over my back, and I spun around to chase her and catch her and bump her shoulder with mine so that we both flopped on the ground. Then I noticed that Burke was rolling down the ramp in his humming chair, so I raced to catch up with him.

He never needed Pull anymore, but there might be *something* I could do.

We headed for the barn, and all the people followed. Lacey came, too, of course. Grant pulled the big barn doors to one side, and Burke stopped his chair to stare.

I sat next to him and stared, too.

There were people in there! Boys and girls! And they were all sitting in chairs with wheels. My nose recognized some of them—they were kids I had met in school. Justin was one of them.

"What's going on?" Burke asked.

Grant pointed. "See the basketball hoop? Dad and I put it up last night."

"Yeah, I see it, but that doesn't mean I *understand* it."

"Regulation height for wheelchair basketball," Grant explained. Justin had one of those big balls sitting on his

lap, and he grinned and threw it toward Burke. At the last moment, Burke put his hands up to catch it.

"Wheelchair basketball?" my boy said.

Grant leaned down. "Oh, and you have to leave the motorized chair behind. The rules say manual only. No Pull from Cooper, either."

Burke frowned back at Grant. "I don't think—"

"Hey," Grant interrupted him. "You were the one who said you wanted to play a sport, right? Well, wheelchair basketball is a sport. You might even be good at this one."

Burke gave him a sour expression. "I've never shot a basket in my life."

"Yeah," Grant agreed cheerfully, "but nobody here has ever been in a wheelchair in their life. Evens the score, don't you think?"

Ava clapped her hands. "This is going to be so much fun!"

Burke glanced at her, then gazed steadily at Grant, who was grinning even more broadly. "I invited Ava," Grant said with a shrug. "Thought it would help raise the stakes."

I was delighted when New Dad wheeled Burke's old chair out from the corner of the barn, and Burke called to me. "Steady, Cooper!"

Steady was my Work. I leaped to Burke's side and braced myself as he put his hand on my back and moved from his humming chair to his other one.

Next, Burke told me to do Pull to the side of the barn, and it felt so good to lean into my harness and take him there. Lacey jumped up on me because she was excited and didn't have a Work to do. I ignored her.

"Stay, Cooper," Burke commanded. Lacey rolled on her back, tongue lolling out, trying to entice me to play, but I was doing Stay.

"Can you hold Lacey?" Wenling asked Ava.

"Sure!" Ava picked up Lacey's leash as Wenling slid into her own chair.

Apparently, Lacey did not know how to do Pull.

Inside the barn, the children began wheeling themselves around. They were awkward and slow, and I would have been willing to do Pull for them, but they didn't ask. They also yelled a lot and threw a ball to each other and sometimes through a metal ring that was attached to one wall of the barn.

I did not really understand what they were doing, but the expression on Burke's face and his laughter told me that he was happy. He was moving much more quickly than everybody else, weaving in and out among the other chairs.

"How does he *do* that?" one of the other boys panted at Grant.

"Practice," Grant told him with a laugh.

The children were somehow having fun without a dog, but I knew it would be even better for everybody if

I got involved. I trembled with the effort of remaining on Stay. Lacey had it easy—her leash was still gripped by Ava, who was clapping and cheering. Finally, my resolve broke, and I ran out among the chairs just as Justin threw the ball to another child, one named Theresa. I leaped up and tried to catch the ball in my mouth, which is the right way to play, but it was too big and popped up into the air. When it came down, it bounced and a girl, one whose name I didn't know, caught it and grinned and threw it into the air so that it fell right through the metal ring. "Thanks, Cooper!" she called out.

I wagged because she'd said my name, and I ran to get the ball again as everybody laughed and some kids called out "No fair!" and "Whose team is Cooper on?"

Ava laughed, too, and she and Lacey ran out to join me. I figured they were going to play, but for some reason, Ava put my leash on me and took Lacey and me back to the side of the barn.

Why get out leashes when everybody was having so much fun? But even though the people didn't seem to understand that ball games are always better with dogs, Lacey and I still couldn't help wagging because all the children were having such a good time. Every time the ball went through the metal ring, there was a lot of shouting, and Lacey and I would bark just so we'd be included.

Sometimes Burke threw the ball through the ring

himself, and sometimes he'd throw the ball to Wenling or the others, who put it through the ring. The children yelled his name a lot, which I liked. When everyone cheered and Grant yelled, "Game over!" I barked because it all seemed so exciting.

Then all the children except Burke stood up!

I'd never seen anyone in a wheeled chair get to their feet before! I was so startled I stared at my boy. Was *he* going to get up, too?

But Burke did not stand up, which was a relief. The humming chair had already brought too many changes to the Farm as it was.

The children talked a little more and laughed, and then they headed out of the barn. New Dad and Grandma followed, and Burke, Ava, Wenling, Lacey, and Grant and I were left behind. Lacey chewed my face, but I ignored her in case I needed to do Work.

"Where did you get all the chairs?" Burke asked.

Grant grinned. "A couple of them are rented, and we got some from garage sales and places like that."

"So you've been planning this for a while?" Burke asked.

"Yeah. It was Wenling's idea," Grant told him.

"Most fun I've ever had," Burke said. "I mean it. Thanks, Wenling. And you were *great* out there!"

All three of them put their arms around each other. Lacey didn't want to be left out, so she jumped up to put her front paws on Wenling's back, and I placed my own paws on Burke's chair so I could be in the middle. Then Ava put her arms around Burke.

We were all doing love.

Then the people wiggled apart, though I would have been happy to stay in that hug all day. A car honked outside, and Wenling said, "That's my dad! Come on, Ava!" and she grabbed Lacey's leash, and she and Ava ran out.

Grant and Burke faced each other. "You were the best, Burke, and some of those players are on the school basketball team. Your shots could use some work, but your passes were great, and man, did you smoke us with your chair. Instead of slowing down the team, you were the reason we *won*."

"It was the most awesome birthday gift *ever*," Burke replied. "Thanks, brother."

"You know where Wenling got the idea? She read about a teen wheelchair basketball league. They play all over, up in the Upper Peninsula, over in Wisconsin, down in Indiana."

"That's cool." My boy nodded.

"So," Grant asked, forcing a casual tone into his voice, "are you going to try out for the team?"

15

We headed back to the kitchen, where the family sat at the table and sang and Burke blew at a cake that Grandma set in front of him. I was not served any of the cake, but I did get some chicken meat that Grandma spooned into my bowl. "You can celebrate, too, Cooper," she told me.

I loved Grandma so much, though I would have preferred some of that sweet-smelling cake.

I forgot all about the cake when Burke put two of those large balls on his lap and drove his humming chair out of the house and down the ramp and out to the barn. He had never played with the big balls before this day. I'd be glad to do Fetch if he wanted me to, but these balls were Grant's, the kind that were too big to go into my mouth.

Burke's old chair, the real chair, was still there, sitting outside. I trotted over and sniffed it, and then Burke told me to do Steady and shifted himself from his humming chair to the real one.

I wagged hopefully. Pull?

"So, Cooper, if I could make the team, it would be the happiest day of my life. And you saw me—I know I'm good at getting around with the ball, and passing it . . . but I have to be able to shoot, too. I have to practice like Grant does."

His voice trailed off. Burke was gazing at something over my head, but then his eyes lowered to mine. "Anyway, it would be against the rules to use my electric wheelchair. So I'm back to manual. You ready to help, Cooper?"

I heard the question and wagged, though I didn't know what he was saying.

He had already set the two balls on the flat cement next to the chair, and now he reached over and picked one up. He held it in both hands, stared at the side of the barn, and then threw the ball in a smooth arc.

It hit the wall and bounced off. Burke sighed. Then he did the same thing with the other ball. I sat down and scratched my ear and watched.

Why weren't we doing Pull? Or Assist? Or Get It? I would even put up with Leave It if that was what my

boy wanted. Why throw balls at a wall that were too big to do Fetch with?

The balls had bounced off the cement and into the grass. Burke wheeled himself over to them and picked them up, one at a time. Then he threw them at the wall again. One bounced off. One swished through the metal ring that I'd noticed before. Both balls bounced away from Burke.

Burke wheeled over to one of the balls, and I went to the other one. I sniffed it and wished I could get it in my mouth to take back to Burke. I used my nose to bump it and rolled it a little bit.

I became as alert as I was when told to do Focus. I couldn't do Fetch on this big ball, but I could *push* it.

"Good boy, Cooper!" Burke exclaimed. He pulled something out of his pocket, and I heard a sound I had not heard in some time—a click! I leaped to Burke's side, and sure enough, he had a treat for me. A click-and-a-treat for doing Push the Ball!

Were we doing Training?

Burke threw the balls again, and this time I ran to one right away. I nosed it, and it rolled in Burke's direction. Push the Ball!

I looked up at Burke, expecting to hear the *click*. But he just shook his head.

"Over here, Cooper," he said. "Get It here to me."

So it wasn't enough to just move the ball. He wanted something else. I wondered what that might be.

"Get It! Get the ball!"

This was frustrating. Get It meant picking it up with my mouth. What did he want me to do with this too-big ball? All I could do was roll it. Roll it . . . toward Burke. Roll it . . . *to* Burke.

Was that it?

I did Push the Ball on that ball, rolling it, steering it as if I were doing Pull Right and Pull Left. I nosed it all the way to his feet, and he laughed with delight.

Click! Treat!

I understood what my boy wanted me to do. He threw the balls over and over, and I nudged them back to him with my nose.

Nothing made me happier than doing Work for my boy.

I was a dog who did Pull to the side of the barn and then Push the Ball as Burke threw it over and over, day after day. Sometimes his tosses fell through the metal ring, but that didn't matter; he still wanted me to roll them back to him.

Soon, he was wheeling himself to one side and another, heaving the balls while still moving. Apparently, doing Pull was not part of this, but I was still on the alert for the bouncing balls and returned them to him instantly.

One night, in bed, I sensed that Burke needed me to sleep close to him. I scooted up so he could put an arm around me. "We go to court tomorrow, Cooper," he whispered to me in the dark. I licked his face. "If we lose, you can't go to school with me ever again. I would *hate* that."

It took a long time for Burke to fall asleep that night. He kept sighing and shifting in the bed, and I kept picking up my head to look at him. At last, he settled down, and I laid my head across his thighs so that we'd be close all night long.

In the morning, it almost felt like a School day. Burke got dressed in a hurry, and everyone was talking a lot and using quick, nervous words. But nobody said, "School," not even Grant, so I was confused. I stuck close to my boy, ready for anything.

At last, everyone hurried out to the truck, and I was relieved to find that my boy needed me to do Steady as he climbed in the back seat. I jumped in to sit between Burke and Grant before anyone could form any ideas about leaving me behind.

It was clear that something was going to happen, and I was going to be with my boy for whatever it was.

Further, the chair New Dad put in the back of the truck was the old one, not the humming one, which meant I was going to be needed to do Work.

We drove to a new building I had never seen before, and we all went inside—Grandma, New Dad, Grant, Burke, and me. We made our way to a room, and there were some people already there, including the woman from the school who smelled like cats and wore such noisy shoes—Ms. Hawkins. I started to go over to her to see if she had any more cheese that she needed my help with, but Burke told me to do Sit and Stay, so of course I did that, instead.

A lady I had not met before came into the room and sat down at a high table. She looked at some papers and moved them around. I scratched my ear.

"So, you've both agreed to this informal mediation instead of a lawsuit," the lady said gravely. She scratched her ear, too. "I'll hear both sides, and this is binding, meaning, my decision is final. Understood?"

New Dad and Ms. Hawkins both said yes.

"Very well. Ms. Hawkins, I'll ask you to go first."

Ms. Hawkins sat up straight in her chair.

"Thank you, Judge," she said. "This dog"—she pointed at me—"is a disruption in my school."

"What kind of a disruption?" the lady asked. "Cooper is his name, is that right?" I wagged for my name and looked at the new lady to see if *she* had any cheese, but she didn't seem to. "Can you give us some examples of how the dog misbehaved?"

Ms. Hawkins seemed a little flustered. "Well. Not exactly. But it's all anybody was talking about."

"*Anyone* being . . ."

"My staff."

"The office staff?"

Ms. Hawkins nodded.

"But I can't see how having the staff in the office talking about Cooper would keep students from learning. Does Cooper bark during class? Or does he seem aggressive in any way?"

Ms. Hawkins shifted in her seat. "Well, no. But it is very distracting for the other students to have such a big animal there. They are always wanting to pet it or talk to it, and of course, that takes away from instructional time."

"The students want to pet the dog," the lady repeated, nodding. "He doesn't act aggressive or threatening, then, or obviously the children wouldn't want to touch him."

Ms. Hawkins frowned. "But the dog isn't *necessary*. That's my point. If a student needs an accommodation for a disability, of course I will provide it. But this student—"

"My son's name is Burke," New Dad interrupted quietly.

Ms. Hawkins compressed her lips. "*Burke* has a

motorized wheelchair that meets all his needs. He can enter the building. He can get from class to class."

"But I can't get up the front steps!" Burke objected.

The lady shook her head. "Mr. Trevino, I must ask you and your son to let Ms. Hawkins finish."

New Dad nodded. "I'm sorry, Judge."

"Please, Ms. Hawkins, go on."

"There's a ramp in the back of the building that allows for wheelchair access," Ms. Hawkins explained. "All of Burke's classes are on the ground floor. Burke doesn't need a service dog at all, and since the animal isn't necessary, I'm within my rights to ban it from the building."

She sat back a little in her chair. It looked as if she was done talking. Everyone seemed tense. I was trying to think what I could do to make everyone happier— lie on my back for a belly rub, maybe?—when the lady who didn't have any cheese nodded. "Very persuasive. All good points."

Grant and Burke exchanged glum glances.

"It would seem, Ms. Hawkins, that on the face of it, banning Cooper makes sense. But I'd like to hear from Burke now and see if he has anything to offer. Can you come up here, Burke, so we can talk?"

"Pull, Cooper," Burke said quietly.

We made our way up to a place near the cheeseless lady's high table.

"Oh, come on, Your Honor," Ms. Hawkins said

peevishly. "This is obviously for show. The boy can clearly wheel around without that dog helping."

"The boy is Burke," New Dad noted testily.

"Enough," the lady at the high table said, holding up her hand. "Both of you are exhausting my patience."

There was a long silence.

"All right, Burke," the lady finally said. "If you don't mind me asking, why are you in a wheelchair?"

Burke nodded. "There was a problem when I was born. An infection, so they had to do surgery. It's why my mom isn't . . . She didn't survive."

"I am so sorry. Thank you for explaining," the lady replied in a quiet voice. "Now, do you want to tell us about Cooper?"

I glanced up at my name.

"First, can I show you this letter?" Burke asked. "It's from Mr. Kindler. He's my history teacher."

The lady nodded. She reached out and took the piece of paper that Burke handed to her and looked at it for a little while. Of all the things humans play with, paper is my least favorite. It smells dry and sticks to my tongue.

"At no point has Burke's service dog disturbed me, the class, or the other students," the lady said, looking carefully at the paper. "He lies quietly by Burke's side. When the bell rings, Cooper sits up but otherwise does not move until Burke gives him a command. Frankly, I wish all my students were as polite as Cooper."

She put the paper down. I glanced over at New Dad. He was smiling.

"Thank you for bringing in Mr. Kindler's letter," the lady said. "Now, Burke, do you agree with the other things that Ms. Hawkins has said? Can you get into school using the ramp and get around once you're there with your motorized wheelchair?"

Burke nodded. "I can, I guess. But Ms. Hawkins doesn't really understand what Cooper does."

"I see," the lady said with a nod. "All right, then, why don't you tell us?"

16

Burke hesitated a moment. He took a deep breath. "Cooper's a service dog, and he helps me with a lot of things—like if I need to get in and out of my chair, or if it's hard for me to get through a sandy place," Burke explained. "But he's more than that. He's an emotional support animal, too."

"The dog isn't properly trained as an emotional support animal," Ms. Hawkins interjected. "A dog like that is supposed to be able to ignore a treat unless it has permission to eat it. This dog can't do that."

"Ms. Hawkins, I will not warn you again," the lady at the high table said sternly. There was another long silence. I yawned. The lady looked down at Burke. "Is what Ms. Hawkins just said true, Burke?"

"Could I show you, Your Honor?"

"Please."

Burke reached into his pocket and pulled out something that smelled delicious. Beef! My body sprang into alertness.

"Cooper. Focus."

I snapped my eyes to him.

Burke tossed the treat on the floor. "Leave It!"

Oh no, not Leave It! Not *now*. But I was doing my Work, so I did Leave It and Focus. The wonderful odor of that treat was in my nose, and I could almost taste it; I wanted it so badly. I licked my lips and waited and waited for Burke to tell me that we were done with Focus and I could have that beef. But he didn't say anything.

I was anxious. What if something happened to that treat while my eyes were on Burke? What if Ms. Hawkins decided to eat it herself? It was so hard not to look.

"Excellent," the lady observed. I felt Burke relax. "Clearly, Cooper can perform as Ms. Hawkins requested."

Ms. Hawkins stirred.

"Cooper, Okay!" my boy told me, and I sprang forward and took the treat in my mouth before anything could happen to it.

"Tell me what kind of emotional support Cooper provides for you," the lady at the high table suggested. I wagged at her when she said my name.

Burke rubbed my chest, and I leaned my head into

his hand with a happy groan. He spoke slowly when he answered the lady. "For one thing, Cooper helps me get up the steps in the morning. All the kids sit together on the front steps before school. It's when we get to see our friends, talk, just hang out. If I didn't have Cooper, I'd have to use the ramp in the back, and I'd miss all that. I'd be all alone in the building, waiting for first bell."

The lady nodded. "I can see how that would be important."

Ms. Hawkins stirred again and made a small noise, and the lady shot her a stern glance.

"Plus, everybody loves Cooper. They all want to talk to him and ask about how I train him and stuff. He's like . . . kind of a passport, I guess."

"A passport? To what?" the lady asked.

"To being just like everybody else. If Cooper's around, I can do everything the other kids do. I don't need anyone to take care of me. I'm just a guy with a dog. And that's all I really want to be."

The lady smiled. "I can certainly understand that. All right, then." The woman wrote some things down on her papers, and no one said anything. Finally, she lifted her head. "Ms. Hawkins, Mr. Trevino."

Ms. Hawkins straightened, and a definite whiff of cat came my way.

"Thank you both for coming this morning. I agree that Cooper is not strictly necessary for Burke to have access to the *building,* but a middle school is more than just walls and a roof, isn't it? There's probably no more important time in the emotional development of children, and they need socialization as much as classroom instruction. What we've seen here today is that Cooper is needed to assist Burke in his personal growth as much as with his mobility."

I wasn't doing Work, and I wasn't getting any more beef. I flopped down with a groan.

The lady chuckled at me. "If I saw any hint that Cooper was aggressive, I'd agree that the school could ban him—indeed, that they should. But, well, look at him. He's a big dog, but he's not a threat in any way."

Ms. Hawkins sighed unhappily.

"Burke, you and Cooper are to be admitted to school starting tomorrow," the lady declared.

"Yes!" Grant shouted. I shot to my feet, and everybody laughed. Well, almost everybody. Ms. Hawkins did not. I thought she was probably sitting there missing her cats, and I contemplated going over to her, but I did not do it. Some people just can't be cheered up, no matter how much attention they get from a dog.

The lady who'd talked to Burke shook hands with him, and then with New Dad and Grandma, and she petted me, too. Ms. Hawkins pressed her lips together in a firm line and strode away from us, holding her head stiffly and taking her cat odors with her.

In the truck going back home, everyone was happy, and I wagged and watched for squirrels. We arrived home, and Wenling and Lacey were there waiting for us! Wenling shouted, "Yes!" just like Grant had, and Burke said, "Okay!" to me, so Lacey and I raced down to the pond to teach the ducks a lesson.

After Lacey and I had wrestled and sniffed and chased, we returned to the pond to find Burke and Wenling on the dock next to Burke's new chair. Burke was lying on his back, and Wenling was sitting up, hugging her knees and looking out across the water.

Lacey flopped down next to Wenling, and I briefly considered lifting my leg against the new chair, but I knew Burke wouldn't like that. So I sat down next to my boy and smelled his hair.

"So you're going to come back to school?" Wenling asked Burke.

"Cooper and me."

"Cool. And soon, we're having the Fall Fling."

"The school dance?" Burke asked.

"Yeah. You want to go?"

Burke turned his head to stare at her. "With you?"

"Well, yeah, since I'm the one sitting here asking you!" Wenling laughed.

Burke hesitated. "Wouldn't you have more fun with someone who can actually dance?"

Wenling rolled her eyes. "Burke, *none* of the boys

can actually dance. Anyway, you're my best friend, and you're the one I want to go with. We'll have fun no matter what."

Burke grinned. "Okay, then. We'll go to the Fall Fling. You and me and Cooper. We'll fling everything that can be flung."

"Wenling!" Grandma called from up at the house. "Your dad called. He'll be here in a few minutes to take you home."

Wenling ran up to the house, and Lacey chased after her. I didn't pursue, because I knew Burke needed me. I did Steady for Burke to slide into his chair. "Go on. I know you want to run with Lacey," he told me. "Okay, Cooper!"

I sprang off the dock and ran after Lacey up to the house. When I caught up to her, I knocked her over, and we rolled in the grass doing play-growls at each other.

Grant had come out onto the porch. "Uh, Wenling," he said. "Can I talk to you?"

Wenling looked over at him. She had Lacey's leash in her hand. "Sure, but I have to grab Lacey," she said. "My dad will be here any minute."

"Yeah. It's just, I wanted to ask you . . . ," Grant said. He rubbed at the back of his head as if he had an itch. "There's that dance at school, right?"

"Sure, the Fall Fling," Wenling said.

Grant took a deep breath. "Do you maybe want to go with me?"

"Oh," Wenling said. I stopped gnawing on Lacey's throat and looked up at the odd note in her voice. She sounded surprised and worried and pleased all at once. "Um, Grant, thanks, but I'm already going with Burke. We'll see you there, though, right?"

"Yeah. Sure," Grant said. A car pulled up in the driveway, and Wenling ran to put Lacey on her leash and pull her away from me. I wished Lacey and Wenling could just stay with us at the Farm all the time. Why did they have to go away?

Grant sighed and went inside the house. I decided he missed Lacey just as much as I did.

A few days after that, we were back in School! I did Assist up the steps and Sit and Stay in the classrooms, just like before, and my friends were all happy to see me. They petted me and talked to me and said my name a lot. "Hey, Burke. Hey, Cooper, you're back!" one kid after another said as we passed in the hallways or sat in the rooms. "Hey, good dog. Cooper, good boy!"

I wagged with happiness, but only Burke knew how to do click-and-a-treat.

"Don't feed him; he's working," Burke would say. I reasoned he was telling them to dig in their pockets and find some chicken, but none of them were smart enough to understand.

Burke did not sit alone at the kitchen table with Grandma anymore. We did School almost every day, and it always made a feeling of satisfaction rise up deep inside me. I was doing Work again, staying close to my boy, there whenever he needed me.

When Burke said, "Focus," it meant more than to just stare into his eyes, I soon learned. It also meant to stop barking. Whenever the doorbell rang, I naturally wanted to alert everyone that there was someone at the door—I knew this, because I could hear the doorbell, and I thought it should be my job to let everyone else know. For some reason, though, as soon as the doorbell chimed Burke always said, "Focus," which meant people wouldn't know there was someone at the door. They would just have to *guess*.

So when the bell rang and Burke said, "Focus," and I smelled Ava on the other side of the front door, I was relieved when he wheeled himself over to open it. Otherwise, poor Ava would have had to stand there all day. I accompanied Burke, of course, and noticed how surprised he seemed when he saw Ava. I wagged because beyond her, out in the driveway, was Old Dad's car, and I could find his scent on the air as well.

"Hi, Burke!"

"Hi, Ava," he replied. "Did you come to visit Cooper?"

I glanced up at my name but felt that I was doing Work and shouldn't go to her unless Burke said, "Okay."

Ava shook her head. "I can only stay a minute."

"Oh."

"So, did you know that if you're in middle school you can ask a fifth grader to the Fall Fling? It's a new rule."

Burke was quiet for a moment. "No, I didn't know that."

"So?" Ava smiled at him.

"Oh! Ava, sorry. I'm going with Wenling to the dance."

Ava's smile crashed. "I thought you were just friends."

Burke nodded. "That's true."

Ava brightened. "Then maybe the *next* dance?"

Old Dad's car horn honked. Ava glanced over her shoulder. "I gotta go. We'll talk soon!"

She ran off the porch, and I twitched, remembering chasing her when I was a puppy, a long time ago, before I learned Work.

Burke shut the door and looked at me. "Seems like I'm getting to be pretty popular," he muttered.

I wagged.

17

I loved the tang of Burke's sweat as we did Work with those too-big-for-my-mouth balls. One sunny afternoon, we were both pretty tired and I was glad to do Pull back to the house. We settled into place in the living room. Burke picked up a long, thin box from the coffee table and clicked a button, and the flat screen started making lights and noise. I settled down next to my boy and put my head in his lap so I could drink in his strong odors.

Grant came out of their bedroom and stared at Burke. "Aren't you going to get ready?" he asked. "It's the Fall Fling tonight. You can't wear that sweaty T-shirt to a dance!"

Burke shrugged. "I don't think I'm going to go."

"What?" Grant stared at him harder.

"I've got a stomachache," Burke said. "I don't think I can make it to the dance."

I heard the sound of a car pulling up in the driveway and ran to the door to greet whoever was arriving. Feet came up the ramp, and I could smell that it was Wenling, so I barked with extra excitement.

But I couldn't find Lacey with my nose. Where was Lacey?

Grandma hurried to open the door and let Wenling inside. "Oh, don't you look lovely!" she exclaimed. "What a beautiful dress!"

Wenling had on something different than her usual pants. Tonight, she was wearing a dress that swished when she walked. I liked the way it moved, but it didn't smell much like Lacey, so it wasn't that interesting.

"Burke's in here. Come on in," Grandma continued, and she and Wenling walked into the living room. "Burke, doesn't Wenling look . . . Burke, what are you wearing?"

"I'm not feeling so good," Burke mumbled. "Sorry, Wenling. I don't think I can go."

"Oh," Wenling said. I could feel disappointment rising off her. Her shoulders sagged, and the excitement in her body vanished. "Oh, I'm . . . I'm sorry you're sick, Burke."

Burke was the only one in the whole room who didn't smell unhappy. He brightened up as if he'd just smelled a treat somewhere. "Hey, I know! Why don't you go with Grant instead?"

Burke looked at Grant. Grandma looked at Wenling. Wenling looked at Grant. I looked at all of them, trying to figure out what was going on that was stirring up such strange moods in the room.

"With Grant? I guess . . . that's a good idea?" Wenling replied a little hesitantly. "I mean, if Grant wants to."

"Um, yeah. I mean, sure, of course I want to," Grant said. He looked down at himself. "Just . . . Excuse me!" He turned and ran into his room.

"Okay, then, good," Burke grunted. He put out a hand, and I nosed it in affection. "You get to go to the Fall Fling after all, Wenling."

"I'm just sorry you don't get to go. I know you were looking forward to it," Wenling replied.

Grandma put her hand on Burke's forehead. "You don't feel hot."

"Probably just a cold," Burke said reassuringly.

Grant was back again very quickly, wearing different clothes that did not smell as nice and sweaty and dirty as the ones he'd had on before. Wenling smiled when she saw him, and he smiled back, and then they both looked away from each other.

"My dad's waiting in the car outside," Wenling said softly, and she and Grandma headed for the door. Grant followed them. He looked at Burke over his shoulder before he left the room.

"Thanks," he said very softly, and Burke waved at him. In a moment, I heard the front door close, and Grandma came back into the room.

"Well," she said, looking at Burke thoughtfully. "I'm sorry to hear you're not feeling so well."

"I'm feeling better already."

"You're a very good brother, Burke. Would you like a glass of ginger ale to help you with your upset stomach?"

Burke grinned at her. "Thanks, Grandma. That'd be great."

"Some pie might help, too."

"That would be even better!"

We did School most days after that and lots of throwing balls through the metal ring hanging off the barn as the air grew colder and the dark seemed to come earlier each day. I remembered what was coming next—snow! And I was right! One day, Grant stumbled to the kitchen door to let me out in the morning, and there was whiteness all over the ground. That afternoon, Lacey and I ran together in the fluffy stuff and bit at it and tossed it over our heads.

After dinner on the day of snow, the whole family

took a car ride—Grandma, New Dad, Grant, Burke, Wenling, and me. I did not know why Lacey wasn't there. I did Steady to help Burke into his seat, and New Dad took his humming chair away. I thought New Dad would put the chair in the back of the truck, as he usually did, but instead, he took it into the house and brought out Burke's *real* chair.

I bounded into the truck with excitement leaping inside me. The real chair! Maybe I'd get to do Pull!

As we drove, new flakes of snow started drifting down from the sky. The truck stopped in a big parking lot. "I can put up the disability sign so you won't have so far to go in the chair," New Dad offered Burke.

"No way," Burke said, putting an arm around me. "I'm not disabled when I've got Cooper."

The car moved again and then stopped, and New Dad brought the real chair around for Burke to slide into. He didn't tell me Assist, but he held my harness as he lowered himself down. I leaped out, and Burke leaned forward and grabbed my leash.

I knew what was coming.

"Cooper, Pull!" he said. The chair's wheels slipped a bit in the wet snow, and I needed all my weight to move it forward. Step by step, we made our way through the parking lot, along a sidewalk, and up a ramp into a building I'd never been in before.

Once inside, I saw that the building was very much

like the school—there were long hallways with lockers on both sides and the smell of many children. But I saw no steps to do Assist on, so it wasn't actually School.

I kept doing Pull down the hallway and into a room that surprised me with its size and noise and smells of people—many, many of them! People were sitting on rows of wooden benches along two sides of the room, and Burke directed me to one of those benches. It reminded me of the same sort of seating when we went to the smelly pond with all the children, but there was no pond here. Burke sat in his chair next to the bottom bench, and I sat next to him, and everyone settled down beside us.

"Good dog," Wenling told me.

I alerted when an older boy in a chair like Burke's, with a big brown dog at his side, made his way over to us. The dog and I stared at each other, and I instantly understood something. This was not a dog like Lacey. This was a dog like *me*. A dog who did Work. "So you're Burke," the boy greeted. "I'm Jeremy, and this is Zeke."

Everyone in the family spoke, saying "Jeremy" and "Zeke" and their own names. I understood that "Zeke" was the dog's name and his boy was "Jeremy."

Jeremy gave Burke a cold stare. "Last year, I was the shooter at halftime. I raised seventy-five dollars for the teen wheelchair league."

Burke nodded. "That's really good."

"But this year," Jeremy continued, "instead of doing tryouts, people got to write an essay. And yours won, even though you aren't on a team or anything."

Everyone was quiet for a moment.

"I'm hoping to try out for the team," Burke finally said softly.

Jeremy gave Burke a tight smile. "Well, you're in luck, because the coach will be out there with you tonight."

"The coach? He's here for the charity?"

"That's right." Jeremy grabbed his wheels. "Good luck."

Jeremy turned, and Zeke gave me a last look before they wheeled away.

"Don't pay any attention to him," Grant murmured. "He's just trying to get inside your head. It's *great* the coach is here. You've gotten really good at this."

Burke nodded, sighing.

There was a long stretch of wooden floor before us, and I noticed that on either end was a metal ring, high up in the air, like the one Burke liked to throw balls at outside the barn. Some boys ran out onto the floor, their sneakers thumping and squeaking against the polished boards. There was a ball, too. A ball! It was as big as the one Burke played with, so I knew what I could do. I looked over at Burke eagerly. Obviously, I should go jump on the ball and nose it back over to Burke. He shook his head at me.

"Sorry, Cooper. Stay," he told me.

Stay is the hardest thing I do for my boy. I love him, so I do my best, but it was so hard to keep my rump on the floor when those boys were running and the ball was bouncing and whistles were blowing and people were yelling. I could feel the excitement of everyone, and it made me excited, too. My tail beat against the floor.

After a while, all the boys ran away, and I figured they were tired from all their playing and were going to take a nap. A man walked out in the middle of the floor and waved at the crowd. He held a stick in his hand, close to his mouth as if getting ready to take a bite out of it. When he spoke, his voice was so loud that it made me twitch all over.

"Thank you, and welcome to North High School!" he boomed. "For those of you who don't know me, I'm Principal MacMillan. Thanks to all who've come out tonight. As you know, it's a special event—we're not just cheering on our basketball team, we're raising money to support a great cause, the teenage wheelchair basketball league, which organizes competitions all over the region. All the proceeds from today's tickets will be donated to the league."

There was more clapping and yelling—I don't know why. Nobody had thrown a ball.

"And now let me turn it over to the president of the local chamber of commerce, Mrs. Brown!"

A woman jogged out from the crowd and joined him. She grabbed the stick. She had a very loud voice, too! "Hello, North High!" she boomed, and everybody clapped again. They seemed to like doing that very much. "Let me introduce Coach Wiley!"

A man in a wheeled chair but without a dog cruised out to sit next to her and wave.

"As you know," she continued, "we're here tonight because the chamber has agreed to donate twenty-five dollars to the wheelchair league for every free throw that local sixth grader Burke Trevino can make tonight, out of three tries. Come on out here, Burke!"

There was louder clapping and yelling than ever, and I looked at Burke in confusion. What was all this noise? He gripped my leash and grinned at me. "Cooper, Pull!"

Pull was much easier on this smooth, wooden floor than it had been outside in the snow. I leaned into the harness and dragged Burke and his chair out into the middle of the big room, next to the woman with the loud voice. Burke said, "Halt!"

I stopped. More of that clapping. Were they going to keep doing that forever?

Someone threw one of those too-big-for-my-mouth balls, which the man in the chair caught and handed to Burke. Burke held it in his lap.

"Glad to meet you, son," the man in the chair greeted.

"I was very impressed with your essay. You really want to be on my team?"

"Yes, sir," Burke replied. "More than anything."

"Well, all right. Let's see what you've got. You think you can make this shot, or should we maybe scoot a little closer?"

"I can make it, sir."

The man in the wheelchair grinned. "Good luck."

18

Burke picked up the ball, eyed the metal ring, and threw it with one hand. It swished through the ring and bounced away along the floor, and I knew just what to do.

The woman with the loud voice had already started moving toward the ball, but I raced past her and nudged it with my nose, turning it around and steering it right back to Burke. All the people made more of that huge noise as Burke leaned down to pick it up.

"That's one for one!" the woman boomed. "Twenty-five dollars!"

I sat patiently. Everyone went quiet. Burke threw the ball, and all the people went crazy with yelling again.

"Two for two!" the woman announced as I ran down the ball and returned it to my boy.

Burke picked it up.

"Last shot!" the woman said to the stick, her voice echoing in the room.

The ball cut through the quiet air and fell through the hoop, and the noise was even louder. I was glad none of these people ever came to the barn to shout, because there Burke would throw the ball all day long.

Then the woman backed up a little and gestured to Burke. "Well," she boomed, "that's seventy-five dollars. Does it look like maybe this is a little too easy for him?"

There was a huge roar in response. I yawned anxiously. The man in the wheelchair grinned.

The lady with the stick moved farther away. "Burke, if you can sink one from here, we'll add in another fifty dollars."

Burke nodded and wheeled himself over to where she was standing. I nudged a ball to him, and he held it in both hands for a moment, then threw it. It swished through the ring.

There was, of course, more loud clapping and cheering.

The woman with the loud voice backed up even farther. "How about here? We'll double the total and donate two hundred and fifty dollars if you can make a basket from here!"

Burke moved the chair again. I pushed the ball over

to him, and he picked it up. "Okay, Cooper," he said softly to me. "This is going to be hard."

The crowd went quiet, and I heard Grant's voice. "You've made shots from farther than that in the barn!" he bellowed.

"You can do it, Burke!" Wenling shouted.

"Just take your time, Burke," the man in the wheel-chair suggested softly.

Burke took the ball in both hands, lifted it, and held it for a few seconds. The people in the stands were utterly silent. Good, I was glad they'd gotten over it.

Burke threw the ball. *Swish!*

I'd been too optimistic to think that the people were done with their noise. I'd never heard so much clapping and stomping and yelling. I ran and retrieved the ball.

"All right!" the woman with the loud voice boomed. "We've got a future NBA star on our hands." She backed up even more, until she was in the middle of the room. "So. Call me crazy, but the chamber of commerce will double the contribution, for a total of five hundred dollars, if Burke can sink a basket from here in midcourt!"

Burke held the ball in his lap and leaned over and grabbed my harness. "Cooper, Pull!" he commanded.

I was glad to do it. I eased my boy up right next to that woman before Burke said, "Halt!"

Again, the people changed their minds and decided

to be quiet. Burke regarded the metal ring. "Oh boy," he muttered.

The woman held the stick away from her mouth. "Good luck," she whispered.

Burke picked up the ball. I watched alertly. "Stay," he told me as if sensing that I wanted to run the second he made his toss. He cranked his arm back, hesitated, and then with a loud grunt heaved it hard into the air.

I twitched, but I was on Stay. The ball soared and soared, going high, and then falling to the floor in front of the ring.

Everyone in the room groaned.

"Tough break," the man in the wheelchair said.

"Okay, Cooper," my boy said dismally. "Get the ball."

I ran and stopped the ball's progress and corralled it back to Burke.

"Well," the woman said in her booming voice. I knew she was capable of being much quieter, but she seemed to prefer being loud. "That was really close! Let's have a big hand for Burke!"

I ignored all the noise and concentrated on nosing that ball next to my boy, who picked it up. He looked at the woman holding the stick. "Could I try one more time?" he asked.

The woman raised her eyebrows. Then she turned to the benches. "He wants to give it another shot!" she thundered.

"A thousand dollars!" someone else yelled.

"Yes! Make it a thousand!"

"A thousand!"

The man in the wheelchair grinned. "We could really use the money," he told the woman holding the stick.

The woman held up her hands. "I think I know a hustle when I see one, but okay. They might fire me for this, but I'm going to say this: we're donating two hundred fifty dollars already, but I'll give this amazing boy and his super dog one more try, and if he sinks it from here . . ." She paused, perhaps enjoying the silence for a moment. "If he makes it from here . . . we'll donate a total of five thousand dollars to the wheelchair league!"

There are a lot of words that are pretty exciting, like *treat* and *walk* and *Pull,* but whatever this woman had just said must have been even better, because the noise from the people on the benches was almost unbearable.

"Wow," Burke said.

The woman grinned. "It's for a charity I believe in. My son wouldn't have gotten a college scholarship if he hadn't played for the wheelchair league. You make this shot, and I'll tell the board members it was just meant to be."

"Okay." Burke took a deep breath and looked down the floor toward the metal ring. I did Sit without being asked. Whatever was happening, I was ready to do Work for my boy.

Then Burke swiveled the chair around so that he was facing away from the metal ring.

The woman with the loud voice laughed. "This I have to see!" she said, and all the people on the benches laughed, too.

The room became as quiet as it had been all night. I could hear people breathing, hear the rustle of their clothing as they shifted on their wooden benches. The tension in the room almost made me quiver— everyone was feeling it.

Burke glanced back over his shoulder at the metal ring. He lifted the ball in both hands and held it. His whole body was still and taut. I fixed my eyes on him. He was nervous, but also happy.

"Okay, Cooper. Here goes."

Burke looked at the ball in his hands, lowered it slowly, and then with a quick motion flung it high and over his head. I watched as it sailed toward the metal ring. First, it bounced off a board, and then it thumped down on the ring itself.

The ball wobbled there on the rim. Everybody in the room sucked in their breath. The ball seemed to hesitate—would it fall inside the ring or outside of it?

Either way, I would go and fetch it. I kept my eyes on the ball. No matter where it went, I was ready.

The ball tipped inward and fell through the ring, bouncing on the floor, and the people on the bleachers *screamed*. I was starting to become accustomed to the idea that they were the sort of people who liked to come to huge empty rooms and yell loudly, but *this* noise really was extraordinary! I didn't let it distract me, though. I ran to the ball and nudged it back over to Burke, and then I put my head in his lap. I felt as if his petting would protect me a little from the sound that was beating at my ears.

Burke rubbed my neck and bent over to put his face in my fur. "I did it, Cooper! *We* did it!" he exulted.

The woman with the loud voice boomed some more, and then Burke told me to do Pull, and we went back to sit with our family.

"Great job, Burke!" Grant said with delight. Everyone hugged my boy and then hugged me.

I was a very good dog.

The boys ran back out to play with the ball some more, and I was content to let them have their turn.

People kept coming up to us to tell me good dog because I'd done Pull and retrieved all the balls. They'd talk to Burke, too, and he'd grin and say, "Thanks!" Some were my friends from School, and they petted me and scratched my ears. I wagged at all of them.

Then someone I hadn't seen in a long time appeared—Ava! And Old Dad! Old Dad talked enthusiastically to

Burke and shook his hand, and Ava threw her arms around my neck and hugged me and planted a kiss on top of my head.

Still hugging me, she looked over at Burke and smiled. Burke's face changed color for some reason, and Grant punched him lightly on the shoulder.

There was a final, loud cheer, and then the boys ran off the floor, and people started standing up and moving. The man in the wheelchair came over to us, as well as Jeremy and the dog Zeke. As before, Zeke and I eyed each other, but we were not the kind of dogs to sniff each other without being told Okay.

"That was some shot," the man in the wheelchair admired. "Is it true you've been practicing all fall?"

"He's out there shooting baskets every day," Grant affirmed.

"It was pretty awesome," Jeremy admitted. "I take back what I said earlier."

"We practice Saturdays and two nights a week," the man in the wheelchair advised. "I'll send you the schedule."

"Can Cooper come to the games? And the practices?" Burke asked. I wagged and swiped at his hand with my tongue because he'd said my name.

"Of course," Jeremy said. "Zeke goes everywhere I go." Zeke wagged for his name. "Looking forward to having you on the team."

The way everyone was grinning alerted both Zeke and me, though no one told us to do anything.

After the two chairs and two people and one dog left, Burke looked over at his family. "Hey, hear that? I'm on the team!"

The family did more of the clapping and stomping. I sat down and sighed. Weren't we done with the noise yet? Grandma hugged Burke, and New Dad hugged Grandma. Then Wenling and Grant hugged each other.

"Hey, I don't know if this calls for a five-minute hug," Burke said, with his eyes on them. "Maybe more like five seconds."

They let go of each other, and Wenling's face changed color, just as Burke's had done earlier.

"Congratulations, Burke!" Ava cried. She hugged Burke even longer than Wenling had hugged Grant.

"Okay. Okay now, Ava," Burke said. "That's good. Okay."

I was hearing, "Okay," but wasn't on Stay, and anyway, Lacey wasn't there to wrestle.

Once we were outside, New Dad looked up at the feathery white flakes floating down from the sky. "It's snowing pretty hard," he said. "I'll go get the car and bring it around."

"Cooper and I will go, too," Burke said.

"I don't know," New Dad told him. "That snow's getting pretty deep."

"Cooper's a sled dog, or half, anyway," Burke said. "That snow's no big deal for him."

He took hold of my leash. Even before he said, "Cooper, Pull!" I was towing him down the ramp and into the parking lot. We headed for the car, with Burke holding on tightly.

I knew then that even if Burke used his new humming chair on most days, even if I didn't get to do Pull as often as I'd like, I still had a purpose, a job. It was what I was meant to do.

I was a dog who did Work.

Reading & Activity Guide to

Cooper's Story: A Puppy Tale

By W. Bruce Cameron

Ages 8–12; Grades 3–7

In *Cooper's Story,* malamute–Great Dane mix puppy Cooper is adopted by fifth grader Burke Trevino's family. Cooper, the pup protagonist, is the narrator. But it is Burke, the story's human main character, who takes the lead in turning the fun, affectionate boy-dog relationship into an amazing partnership, which helps them both discover new purpose and potential. With the support of family and friends, determined Burke takes it upon himself to train Cooper to be his service dog and emotional support animal, so Burke can attend sixth grade at his local middle school. Burke does not let being paraplegic or any logistical or legal obstacles stand in his way. Burke successfully trains Cooper to be a skilled working service dog, and, with his dog and his family in his corner, Burke fights for a full and fair place in his school and larger community, academically, socially, and athletically. With many uniquely compassionate connections, between brothers, friends (human and canine), and family members, *Cooper's Story* is truly a tale about the power of love, loyalty, and focusing on what you can do instead of what you can't do. And, for Cooper, helping his boy find his way in the world also helps Cooper find his place in it.

Reading *Cooper's Story: A Puppy Tale* with Your Children

Pre-Reading Discussion Questions

1. Cooper is more than just a beloved pet for fifth grader Burke. Cooper also becomes his service dog. Do you have experience, or know someone who has experience, with a service or support animal? From that experience, what do you know about how service animals are trained, and how they interact with the person they help, as well as with other people they encounter while they are "on duty"?

2. Have you ever had a special pet that helped you in unexpected or important ways? Or have you observed a friend or family member who had a unique relationship with a pet? What was special or powerful about those pet-person connections?

3. In *Cooper's Story*, people and pups form strong bonds with each other, but there are special relationships that develop between animals, too. In fact, Cooper has a "BFF" (best furry friend, maybe even girlfriend) named Lacey. Living in the same shelter, though they are from different litters, Cooper and Lacey have been fast friends since their earliest days. Have you

observed or read about friendships that were unusually strong or special between animals? What animals were involved, and what was unique about the relationship?

Post-Reading Discussion Questions

1. Canine narrator Cooper opens the story with his dog's-eye view of the world. What are the first things you learn about from his puppy perspective? Do you think a human narrator's introduction to Cooper's environment, family, caretakers, and favorite pup playmate would be similar or different? How?

2. Even though Cooper has brothers and sisters, he is closest to Lacey, who is a pup from another litter. Ava, who helps her father care for dogs and puppies in need of forever homes, observes Cooper's special bond with Lacey. In Chapter 1, Ava says to Cooper: "Lots of people have true loves. . . . So I don't see why dogs shouldn't. Even puppies." Do you agree that a dog can have a true love, just like a person? Why or why not?

3. Even though Cooper doesn't speak human language, he is very good at picking up clues, especially through his senses, which help him interpret what humans are feeling. For example, on adoption fair day, Cooper observes of Ava: "Her excitement hummed off her skin. It made her voice high and eager." Can you cite some other examples from the story where Cooper

senses certain emotions in his human companions? Can you remember some of the specific sensory details—sights, sounds, or smells—that he picks up on and what they signal?

4. In Chapter 2, Cooper is dejected after Lacey and his siblings and mother dog are adopted by families and he is left alone, but then he meets his adoptive family. The younger brother, Burke, uses a wheelchair and explains that he plans to train Cooper to be his service dog. What are some of the concerns Ava's dad has about the service dog idea?

5. When Cooper arrives at his new home at the Farm where New Dad, Grandma, Grant, and Burke live, he thinks: "I could choose right there, I realized, between my normal life with Lacey and a new life here in this strange place." Can you relate to the conflict Cooper is experiencing between being open to something new and wanting to return to what is known and familiar? Can you think of a situation you have experienced where you had to pick between trying something new or sticking with what was familiar?

6. In Chapter 3, running on the farm property, Cooper observes: "Soon I found myself at the top of a small hill, where grass rolled smoothly down to a giant puddle, the biggest I'd ever seen." He doesn't realize that the "giant puddle" is a pond because he hasn't seen a pond before. Can you think of other examples from the story where Cooper's limited frame of reference

or dog's-eye view make his description of an object or interpretation of a situation humorous?

7. In Chapter 4, Burke explains that he needs to do a lot of socialization work with Cooper. Why is this so important? How do Ava, Old Dad, and Grant and his friends all help with socializing Cooper?

8. In Chapter 5, Burke's friend Wenling visits and Cooper is delighted that she is the girl who adopted Lacey. As Burke and Wenling are chatting, the subject of Burke's disability comes up and Wenling says she knows Burke doesn't like to talk about it. He says: "No, it's okay. I don't mind anymore. It's like training Cooper has changed things." What do you think Burke means by this? How and why do you think working with Cooper is changing how Burke feels about himself?

9. At the end of Chapter 6, Cooper thinks: "I loved Burke the most, because I had a sense that he *needed* me in a way the others didn't. Fulfilling that need was my purpose." Why do you think it is important for Cooper to understand his purpose? Having a clear purpose is important for a person, too. Can you think of an important role, or purpose, you have in your home, family, school, or community? How and why is it important to you?

10. Once Cooper is good at performing commands, Burke says he's ready to be tested in real-life situations. Burke says: "It's time to get serious. Cooper needs to learn to work." What does Burke mean by this? And what are some of the ways he tests Cooper

and helps him make the transition to "doing work"? What difficult choice does Cooper have to make in Chapter 8, when the gruff dog Colonel challenges Lacey at the same time Burke calls Cooper to come to him? What does Cooper learn from this situation?

11. In Chapter 11, how does the first day of school go for Burke and Cooper? Does all of their hard work pay off?

12. What is the big surprise (organized by Grant and Wenling) Burke gets on his birthday in Chapter 14? How does it help him finally figure out a sport that might be a good fit for him to try? And do you think Grant is right to keep trying to encourage Burke to try a sport? Why or why not?

13. At the mediation in Chapter 15, the mediator decides in favor of Burke being allowed to bring Cooper back to school, and against middle school principal Ms. Hawkins who thinks Cooper should not be at the school. The mediator concludes that Burke needs Cooper to help him with his personal growth as much as his mobility and should be allowed at school. Do you agree with the mediator's decision? Why or why not? Explain your answer.

14. In Chapter 17, Burke pretends to be sick and unable to take Wenling to the Fall Fling. He suggests Grant take her instead. Do you think Burke makes the right choice to feign illness so Grant can take Wenling? Why or why not?

15. In Chapter 18, after successfully shooting baskets from his wheelchair and winning a big contribution to the teenage wheelchair basketball league, Burke says to Cooper: "I did it, Cooper! *We* did it!" Burke and Cooper certainly worked together to achieve things, but what did their special partnership teach each of them about their individual identities?

16. In this story, author W. Bruce Cameron is very straightforward and open in discussing Burke's disability. Do you agree this is the best way to tackle a subject that can sometimes be sensitive or difficult to discuss? Did this story make you think differently about physical abilities or disabilities?

Post-Reading Activities

Take the story from the page to the pavement with these fun and inspiring activities for the dog lovers in your family.

1. In *Cooper's Story*, Burke trains Cooper to perform tasks that help him in his daily life. Burke needs special assistance because he uses a wheelchair. Dogs can help people with physical or emotional needs in lots of different situations. Are there commands or tasks you could train a family dog to perform (or partner up with a friend who has a dog, if you don't have one) that might be helpful to you or a family member or friend? If so, you can follow some of the

training methods Burke used with Cooper to get a dog to help someone get more exercise, get their slippers, or even just smile, laugh, and de-stress a bit by watching a dog do some clever, fun tricks. (Remember, in addition to being a service dog, a big way Cooper helped Burke was by just being a fun, friendly, loving dog.)

2. Cooper begins life at a shelter. Together with a family member, research animal rescue organizations or shelters in your area. Are there volunteer opportunities you could get involved in with a family member? Or find out if there are other ways you can help the animals in need. You might gather with animal-loving friends to make dog-friendly treats, toys, or blankets and donate them to the shelter.

Reading Cooper's Story in Your Classroom

These Common Core–aligned writing activities may be used in conjunction with the pre- and post-reading discussion questions earlier in this section.

1. **Point of View:** Cooper's best friend, boxer pup Lacey, is a big part of his life and his story. Virtually inseparable in their early days at the shelter, the two joyfully reunite when their owners (Burke and Wenling) turn out to be best friends. All we know about Lacey comes from Cooper's perspective. But what is Lacey's point of view? Have students write two to three paragraphs from Lacey's perspective.

How does she recall meeting Cooper and their early puppy days together? What did it feel like to be adopted by Wenling and have a girl of her own? How would she describe her separation from, and reunion with, Cooper? Consider how author W. Bruce Cameron embraced a dog's-eye view of the world to create a candid, authentic voice for Cooper, as you try to give Lacey a vivid, believable voice of her own.

2. **Brotherly Love:** The Trevino brothers in *Cooper's Story* have a relationship that is in some ways very typical and in other ways unique. Grant and Burke joke and tease, share a room, and irritate each other like many older/younger brother pairs. But their dynamic also reflects the loss of their mother and the extra physical challenges Burke has to navigate since a complication at birth left him disabled. Their brotherly banter is filled with mock insults and putdowns, but beyond the juvenile jokes and chronic ribbing, it becomes clear throughout the story that they most definitely have each other's backs. Invite students to write a one-to-two-page essay that explores the relationship between Grant and Burke. Include examples from the text about how they support and encourage each other, how they appreciate each other, and how they show, through their actions—which are far more representative of how they feel about each other than their often goofy or teasing words—how much they will do to help, support, and be there for each other.

3. **Text Type: Opinion Piece.** Burke does the research and puts in the work to socialize and train Cooper to be an effective service dog. Cooper's physical and emotional support proves to be a critical factor in helping Burke navigate middle school both physically and socially. However, Ms. Hawkins, the middle school principal, is concerned about having Cooper at school because he was not professionally trained to be a service dog through a certified training program. She argues that Cooper is a distraction to other students at the school and suggests that he could be a safety risk because he is such a large dog. And when Burke gets a new motorized wheelchair, Ms. Hawkins asserts that Burke does not even need Cooper to assist him in getting around at school. In your opinion, is Ms. Hawkins right that Cooper should not be allowed at the school, or do you think Burke is right that Cooper has the training, disposition, and socialization to remain? Write a one-page essay explaining why you think Cooper should or should not be allowed to accompany Burke to school as his service dog even though he was not professionally trained. Include details and examples from the text to support your argument.

4. **Text Type: Narrative.** Though she may seem like more of a background character in the story, Grant and Burke's grandma plays a key role in their home and family. In the character of Grandma, write the story of Cooper joining the household. How does

it change life on the farm to have the bighearted, big-pawed pup in the mix? Include his homecoming, training, and evolution into a reliable service dog and invaluable companion for Burke. How does Cooper's role change when Burke gets a new motorized wheelchair, and again when Burke decides to try out for the wheelchair basketball league? If you had to pick a favorite moment or accomplishment you witnessed Burke and Cooper sharing, what would it be?

5. **Research & Present: Service Dogs & Emotional Support Dogs.**

In *Cooper's Story*, Burke trains Cooper to be his service dog. As they live, work, and play together, Cooper becomes his emotional support dog, too. Just as Cooper supports Burke, dogs can provide vital physical, logistical, and emotional support to individuals dealing with a wide range of illnesses, disabilities, and physical and mental health challenges. Service dogs, emotional support dogs, and therapy dogs play different, critical roles in helping people lead full and happy lives, in spite of extra challenges they might have to navigate. Go to the library or online to learn more about the training, work, and life-changing skills and services of these amazing dogs. (**HINT:** Check out the **American Service Dog Association** at americanservicedog.com and the **Alliance of Therapy Dogs** at therapydogs.com.) Use your research to create a PowerPoint or other multimedia-style presentation to share with your classmates.

6. **Research & Present: Adaptive Sports.**

In *Cooper's Story,* Burke wants to participate in a sport. There some ups and downs in his search, but, ultimately, he figures out that wheelchair basketball might be just the right fit. Like Burke, many people of all ages want to be able to enjoy the fun, camaraderie, and health benefits of exercise and sports, in spite of physical limitations or challenges they may have. Fortunately, there are many terrific resources and opportunities available for athletes with disabilities. Adaptive sports allow modifications that make it possible for athletes to participate fairly and fully in recreational or competitive settings. In pairs or small groups, do some online and library research to learn more about the world of adaptive sports, which offers opportunities from basic fun play up to the Team USA Paralympic athletic level. (**HINT:** Check out **Move United** at moveunitedsport.org or **Team USA U.S. Olympic & Paralympic Committee** at teamusa.org/About-the-USOPC/Paralympic-Programs.)

You might also choose to learn more about wheelchair basketball, which is the sport Burke decided to pursue. (**HINT:** Check out the **National Wheelchair Basketball Association** at nwba.org.) Present your research to classmates in oral presentations. Create an informative booklet about adaptive sports to accompany your presentation. If possible, make copies to share with classmates. If possible (and with permission), you might leave copies of the booklet at your local library, gym, doctor's office, and so on, to make people throughout your community aware of adaptive sport resources.

Supports English Language Arts Common Core Writing Standards: W.3.1, 3.2, 3.3, 3.7; W.4.1, 4.2, 4.3, 4.7; W.5.1, 5.2, 5.3, 5.7; W.6.2, 6.3, 6.7; W.7.2, 7.3, 7.7

About the Author

W. BRUCE CAMERON is the #1 *New York Times* best-selling author of *A Dog's Purpose*; *A Dog's Journey*; *A Dog's Way Home*; *A Dog's Promise*; the Puppy Tales, including *Ellie's Story, Bailey's Story,* and many more; and the Lily to the Rescue chapter book series. He lives in California.

www.BruceCameronBooks.com